# Huntress
## OF THE Sea

# ALAN TEMPERLEY

# HUNTRESS OF THE SEA

SCHOLASTIC

Scholastic Children's Books,
Commonwealth House, 1-19 New Oxford Street,
London WC1A 1NU, UK
a division of Scholastic Ltd
London ~ New York ~ Toronto ~ Sydney ~ Auckland
Mexico City ~ New Delhi ~ Hong Kong

First published in the UK by Scholastic Ltd, 1999
This edition published by Scholastic Ltd, 2002

ISBN 0 439 98258 8

Typeset by DP Photosetting, Aylesbury, Bucks
Printed and bound in Great Britain by Cox & Wyman Ltd, Reading, Berkshire

10 9 8 7 6 5 4 3 2 1

# Contents

*For my parents*
*Fred and May Temperley*

# Chapter One

# The Ragged Man

I had left the school bus at the road-end and was walking home over the hill when I saw him again. It was dusk, for the month was February, but I saw him plain enough: a man aged thirty-five or forty with rough black hair, a scrubby beard and a bad cough. His clothes were dirty. A navy-blue jacket, burst at the shoulder, hung open though the air was bitter. He stood, or half hid rather, by a patch of whins above the road, looking down on me.

I hurried along, schoolbag bumping on my back, and pretended to take no notice. But as the road twisted past bogs and rocky outcrops, he kept pace above me. From boulder to boulder he flitted, jacket flapping, and at length dropped down to the road fifty metres behind.

"Ewan!" How did he know my name? "Ewan McKenzie. Stop!" Cough – cough – cough. He put up no hand. "Come here a minute."

But I certainly was not stopping for a ragged man I didn't know, on a lonely part of the road and a dark evening of the year. I began to run. I don't run fast, indeed I run and walk with a limp for the muscle of my left leg was damaged when I was younger. The stranger began to run too, but though he was bigger and much stronger, he was in poor shape and soon fell behind.

"Ewan!" His voice reached me above the wind that began to blow in my face as I reached the crest of the moor. "Wait. Wait for me."

But I was not waiting and ran on down the broken road. Below me, half a mile off yet, lay the croft house where I lived with my mother, and scattered round the bowl of the hills half a dozen more houses with lights shining cheerfully from the living-room windows. Beyond lay the beach and cliffs and grey sea.

As the road descended the man was lost behind me and five minutes later I pushed open the door of our house, which was seldom locked, and turned the key behind me with relief. I slung my bag into a corner and hurried to the window. Standing there, I pulled off my anorak and rubbed the chill sweat from my forehead. There was no sign of the stranger. Then I saw him, above the road again and trudging across the hillside. Several times he paused, hunched up and coughing. Soon he reached a vantage point, a sheltered spot I knew well, with a fine view across the glen. Clutching the collar of his jacket to the throat, he sank down between some thorns and a dry stone dyke.

Our collie, Fly, was barking from the shed. I let her out and made a fuss of her as she jumped up, panting in my face. We returned to the house together.

My mother, I guessed, would be visiting Peter and Johnina, who had a croft above the shore. This being Tuesday, she'd have collected some messages for the old couple and stopped on for a blether. I drew the curtains, switched on the light and rang their number:

"Hello, Johnina. It's Ewan. Can I speak to Mum?" She came on the line. "... Yeah, fine. Look, that man's here again. He chased me down the road. . . Yes, he's up there by the old dyke now, watching. . . I locked it when I came in. Will you be long?"

Two or three minutes later Mum's old Fiesta came rattling over the cattle grid at the gate. I ran out to meet it. She had brought Magnus with her, Johnina's middle-aged son. For as long as I can remember he had wanted to marry my mum. His chances were nil.

"Are you sure, Ewan?" Mum's dark eyes roamed the hillside. "Where is this man?"

"He was right there, in that corner." I pointed. "I think he spotted the car 'cause he suddenly jumped up and climbed away over the dyke."

"You two go on into the house." Magnus hitched up the thick belt he wore on top of his overalls. "I'll go after him."

"Not a bit of it." Mum was so used to herding our sheep she crossed the moors like a stag, much faster than the lazy unemployed Magnus. "Just let me get a stick."

In a minute she was ready, changed into boots. "Right, we'll go up the burn. Ewan, put the kettle on. There's pancakes in the tin and a Battenberg in the car. I'll make dinner after."

"Mum, can I no' –?"

"Not this time, Ewan. Be a good boy. We'll be back in half an hour." The scars down the side of her face were dark in the fading light. "Right, Magnus. See if we can find out who the man is. I won't have him frightening Ewan like this."

With a swirl of her skirt she started up the steep track by the burn that runs past our house. Magnus, ten years older and overweight, followed in her wake.

But the man was nowhere to be seen.

"I'll ask at the Clachan Inn," Magnus said as he set off after tea and cakes.

"You get yourself away home," Mum scolded him. "If you didn't waste all your money in that pub you'd be able to buy a car."

"Aye, aye." Magnus patted his stomach. "But it's the walking keeps me fit. Ta-ta."

Mum laughed and we went back inside.


"What a rate you're growing, Ewan. These jeans were too long a couple of washes back; now I'm letting down the seam." They were an old pair I liked wearing, with a paint stain and a torn back pocket. Mum stretched out the leg and looked at it critically.

It was later that same evening. Dinner was over and we sat in the living-room. As she picked at the threads, Mum half watched TV over the top of her glasses. I was drawing a map for homework.

The fire had burned low. The last shell of peat collapsed in a shower of sparks. Mum took a sip of coffee and reached towards the peat bucket but it was empty.

"Oh, Ewan, nip out and fill the bucket will you."

"Right." I finished shading the edge of the Mediterranean and set down my felt-tip.

The wind had risen. As I pulled on a jacket I became aware of it rushing round the house. The loose sheet of tin on the shed roof was banging.

Fly was ahead of me in the hall. Suddenly she froze, snarling, and backed away from the front door. Twice she barked then slunk back into the living-room, tail between her legs.

"What's wrong with Fly?" called my mother. "Got the spooks again?"

"I've no idea," I said. "I hope it's not that man still hanging around."

"Oh, Ewan! This is not like you." My mother joined me and took up her shepherding stick that stood in the hall. I switched on the outside light and cautiously opened the door.

No one stood on the threshold. We went out. The stony drive, the wintry grass and vegetable patch, were deserted.

"Maybe it's that roof bothered her," said my mother. "I'll fix it tomorrow." She hugged arms about her shoulders. "Oh, it's parky!" She went back inside.

A northerly wind, blowing off the sea and carrying a fine drizzle, hit me in the face. The three pines which give some shelter to our peat stack at the gate, shook shaggy branches. It was a sight I had seen a thousand times but this night, after my scare coming home from school, it seemed creepier than usual. I stared all round, prepared for flight, and checked behind the peat stack in case the stranger was lurking there. He wasn't. Crouching then, I filled the bucket with hard black peats.

Suddenly, above the soft roar of the sea and swish of wind in the trees, I heard another sound, sharp and dry.

Cough – cough!

My heart leaped. I whirled to face the house. Midway between me and the door stood the stranger, silhouetted against the light. His arms hung at his sides, his shoulders and hair glistened with raindrops.

"Ewan." He took a step towards me.

"Mum!" I dropped the bucket and retreated behind the peat stack. "Mum!"

"Ewan!" He waved his hands to silence me. "No!"

"Mum!"

There was a swift movement within the house. The door was flung open and my mother ran out.

"Ewan, what is − ?" The words died on her lips.

The stranger turned towards her and made a sort of helpless gesture with his arms.

"Jessie?" His voice was uncertain.

My mother's expression changed. "Duncan?" It was barely a whisper. She stepped backwards and put a hand to the wall for support. Then her legs gave way and she fell senseless to the wet ground.

# Chapter Two

# Black Dog

I had no memory of my father, and the tramplike figure with wild eyes who sat on a newspaper at the kitchen table was very strange to me. In two details I was like him: the thick dark hair and blue eyes, unusual with such colouring. But he bore little resemblance to the framed photograph that lay beneath pillowcases in a drawer in my mother's bedroom. The young man in the photograph was smiling, handsome, determined, as any man would have to be who won the hand of Jessie Mackay. But this man, with his deep racking cough and the sweat standing on his forehead, appeared half mad. He was unable to sit still. His head twitched. His fingers gripped now the table, now his knees, now his upper arms. Constantly, as if pursued, he glanced behind.

Fly, a good-natured dog, was terrified of him. On his arrival she had backed snarling, then darted at his legs to attack him – or protect us. Now she had retreated to the furthest corner of the living-room and lay on the carpet behind Mum's chair, watching with anxious eyes.

"Seven years!" My mother lifted bacon, black pudding and potatoes from the stove and set them before him. "Seven years, Duncan! Never a word. And you turn up like this on a cold winter's night." Angrily she sat at the head of the table. "Look at you! What's Ewan to think? What am I to think?"

The man – it was hard to think of him as my father – regarded her with those striking eyes fringed with dark lashes. He trembled. Then his nostrils – I saw it – flared at the scent of the food. Looking down, he took a potato in one brown hand and a rasher of bacon in the other. Head thrusting forward, teeth white and chewing with his mouth open, he devoured them like an animal.

I glanced at my mother.

"Duncan," she said. "I don't know how you've been living, or where, but in this house you'll use your knife and fork like a civilized man."

"How I've been living!" A wild laugh broke from him and was instantly checked. "Sshhh!" Intently he listened and looked all round. "No."

He returned to his plate. Clumsily with knife and fork he pulled the black pudding to pieces. Elbows on the table, he raised his cup of tea with both hands.

I stared at his fingernails. They were thick, like a labourer's, and filed to a point, almost like claws.

Abruptly he was racked by a spasm of coughing. The tea spilled over his hands.

"It's so hot in here!" He tugged at his collar. "No air!"

His jacket hung dripping in the hall. Now he peeled off his ragged jersey. As he did so the T-shirt he wore beneath was dragged up his back. There was not a spare ounce of flesh upon his body. His skin, I saw with astonishment, was brown as leather, burned by the sun or beaten by the salt wind, and covered with scars, some old, others more recent. Mum saw it too. We said nothing.

He finished his meal and hacked a crust from the new loaf.

"Ewan," my mother said. "Away upstairs. This man and I have to have a talk. We'll not be long. I'll give you a call." She nodded towards the door in a manner that meant there was no arguing. "And play some of your tapes, I don't want your ear stuck to the floor."

Reluctantly I left the table and eased past the man who sat between me and the door. A strong stink rose from him – sweat or fish oil or rank seaweed, I couldn't place it. He stretched out an arm.

"Have you no' a hug for your long-lost father?"

Was it affection or a bitter joke – I had no idea. Either way it repelled me and I shrank back. My expression must have mirrored my feelings for his arm fell.

"Away to your room now, Ewan," said my mother.

I pulled the kitchen door shut behind me. Fly crept from behind the chair, looking for reassurance. I patted her and, though it was against the rules, took her upstairs with me. Reliving every moment of the scene below, I lay on my bed. Then angrily, to swamp my feelings, I thrust my favourite loud tape into the player and turned up the volume.

Minutes passed. Suddenly, above the beat of the music, I heard a noise downstairs; the crash of something breaking and raised voices. I switched off the cassette and ran out to the landing.

Phrases reached me:

"... so beautiful was she ... before you knew me ... and now you dare..."

My father's voice intervened: "... don't understand ... not like that! Listen to me! ... can't help it, they..."

"... thought you were dead ... come back here like a savage ... how upset Ewan is..."

"... think I wanted to ... terrible things, terrible ... dead men, bones ... all that time I..."

"... not enough for you? ... have stayed away! ... don't touch me!"

Then there was a scream and another crash, heavier this time as if something had fallen.

I raced downstairs and through to the kitchen. A chair lay on its side, my mother was picking herself from the floor. My father stretched out a hand to help her.

"No!" she cried. "No! I'm all right. Leave me alone. Don't touch me!"

The chair was righted. To cover the awful moment Mum began clearing the table. My father hovered, moving things towards her, then sat down again on the damp newspaper.

I crossed to the sink. "Are you all right?"

"Yes, just a little accident." She gave me a tight smile and put an arm round my shoulders. "Nothing to worry about, Ewan, love. Go and talk to your father."

I sat at the table but couldn't think of anything to say. Nor for a while could he. My mother, her back resolutely turned, clattered dishes in the washing-up bowl.

"You're limping," my unshaven father said at length. "What have you done to your leg? Twisted it at football?"

"No, it – " I looked to the sink for help.

"I'll tell you what happened to his leg." Mum turned abruptly, her fingers covered with foam, wiping away tears with a wrist. "The same thing as happened to my face." She turned her scarred cheek and brow towards him. "The very day you vanished, Duncan McKenzie."

A terrible look of hurt and tenderness crossed my father's face. "Oh, Jessie! I don't know what to say. And you used to be so bonny!"

If he could have spoken crueller words, though unintentional, I do not know them. Stricken, my mother stared at him. But if Jessie Mackay had been the prettiest girl in that part of the country, she had also been one of the most spirited. As I saw her struggling with her feelings I hated my father and wished him dead, wished he would go back to wherever he had come from and never return.

"Yes, I was bonny." My mother's head came up, her back straightened. "Thank you for reminding me, Duncan." Wiping her fingers on the dishcloth, she stood at the table. "Let me tell you what happened. Let me tell you exactly, the day you abandoned us for your – adventures."

The events of that morning as my mother recounted them were truly horrific. I knew the story well, but since I had been only a boy of five at the time, what I actually remembered and what I had been told had become mixed.

It was late summer and all through the glen people had been disturbed by a howling in the night. Before morning it ceased and when my father set off for the shore, striding down the glen to set his creels, the day seemed peaceful. Then Johnina telephoned to say that one of their cattle had been killed in the pasture and part eaten by some big animal.

As my mother took the call, I was playing around the barns in the sunshine with Fly, who was just a pup then. Suddenly – I can remember this much clearly – Fly gave a frightened yelp and shot back towards the house. Surprised, I looked up and saw a huge dog watching me from the end of the barn. It was the biggest dog you ever saw, the size of a calf, shaggy and jet black with yellow eyes. It snarled, showing savage teeth, and came leaping towards me.

My mother tells me I screamed. She dropped the phone and ran, tripping over Fly who came scuttling in through the door. As she rounded the corner of the barn the black dog had me by the leg and was dragging me off across the moor. She shouted and grabbed a spade that leaned against the barn. The brute stopped and looked back then shook me the way a normal dog shakes a rabbit and dropped me in the heather. Brandishing the spade, Mum ran towards it. The dog waited, its mouth red, then sprang at her. A huge claw raked the length of her face. But Mum, seeing me threatened, was as fierce as the dog itself. She fought back. Time and again the spade struck it across the neck and ribs. Thick blood matted its coat and reddened the heather. Then the spade hit one of the dog's front legs. With a yowl the beast jumped back. Again my mother slashed at it. Turning tail, the black dog as big as a calf ran off across the moor on three legs, one paw hanging.

My mother then turned to me. I was unconscious, my leg twisted and torn. She picked me up, her blood mingling with mine, and carried me back to the house. But as she looked down at the ground – and this is very strange – the blood of the creature was nowhere to be seen; the blade of the spade, which had been scarlet and wet, was streaked with dry earth, no more, exactly as it had been when she grabbed it from the wall of the barn. It was as if the black dog had never existed.

Our wounds were real enough, however. I was a month in hospital and ever afterwards walked with a limp. And my mother's face and many other bites and scratches were cleaned and stitched, but Jessie McKenzie, the prettiest young wife for twenty miles around, was scarred for life.

"And that was the day you disappeared," she told my father as we stood that windy night in the kitchen of our old croft house. "The day you sailed off in your boat with– " she glanced at me and bit the words back – "and everyone thought you were drowned." She returned to the sink and began drying the dishes. "And if anyone tells me the two events are not connected, Duncan, I won't believe them."

My father's gaze turned from her face to my legs and then to the curtains as a fierce gust flung raindrops against the window. A cloud of ash puffed from the dead fire.

"It's getting cold, Ewan," Mum said. "Away out for those peats now. Dry ones from the back."

The stranger – my father – rose. "No, I'm wet already. Rain doesn't bother me. Where's the bucket?"

"Where I dropped it," I whispered.

The house lights flickered as lightning struck nearby, followed instantly by a rip and long rumble of thunder.

He left the room. The front door shut behind him.

My mother and I looked at each other. Neither of us could find anything to say. She poked the ash from the grate and went to the cupboard below the sink.

"I'll put on a couple of firelighters."

As she returned she froze, packet in hand. Above the wind and rattling windows there was a new sound outside – my father's voice raging in the storm. Then he gave a howl that made my skin shiver and the hairs prickle on my neck. It was like the cry of some tormented animal and I was frightened.

Was this man really my father? And was he home for good?

# Chapter Three

# The Naked Swimmer

My mother dumped my father's clothes in a bin-bag and insisted that he took a hot bath with Dettol in the water. Then she made up a bed for him on the settee in the living-room.

I slept badly that night and each time I woke heard my father stalking restlessly about the room below, muttering and exclaiming aloud to himself.

The storm subsided and the next morning, though she was very strict about attendance, my mother kept me from school.

"You're white as a sheet, Ewan," she told me as we sat with my father, wrapped in a blanket, at breakfast. "Someone's sure to ask what's wrong – and anyway, I want you with me today."

While I washed the dishes she made a bonfire and burned my father's rags. Then she and I drove into town and bought him a complete new set of clothes; also a hairbrush, toothbrush and razor.

He looked much better after that, especially when he had trimmed straight his oddly-pointed nails, shaved off his black whiskers and allowed my mother to cut the tangled hair that hung past his ears.

Shorn and tidy, it was just possible to see that my father had once been the young man in the photograph. Indeed he was handsome, although painfully thin. He was strong too, for the muscles of his arms were ridged and hard. But none of this hid the wildness in his eyes – those blue, animal eyes fringed with dark lashes – or the ever-present fear. At the least crack of a board or rustle in the grass, his head spun round and when he looked back he was trembling.

Two years previously my mother's father had died and left her his boat, a sturdy five-metre rowboat with an outboard motor. It was called the *Kittiwake*. Freshly painted and overturned for the winter, it lay on chocks above the jetty.

After a few days my father, who was too shy to meet the local men – though his return had caused a sensation and we had many callers – was eager to take the boat to the water. His cough was better and time hung heavy on his hands. Many times he appealed to my mother without success. At length, reluctantly, she agreed.

"But don't think Ewan's going with you. Are you listening, Ewan? Never! I'm not going to risk losing my son as well as my husband."

So the *Kittiwake* was rolled on logs to the water and tied up at the jetty.

It was early March, a stormy season of the year, and my father was the only local man courageous or foolhardy enough to go fishing at that time. Sudden squalls blew in from the north with flurries of snow. Freak waves rounded Roan Island, three miles out, exploded against our cliffs and swilled back, forming treacherous cross-currents. My father, however, was a remarkable fisherman, and every time he went out he returned with a fine haul of cod, haddock and lobsters. Some we sold, some we ate and some, in a white enamel bucket, I carried round to neighbours as gifts. It won him approval, though his sudden return and wild look continued to excite speculation.

One morning – it was Saturday – I thought I would follow him along the coast, hiding behind rocks and wearing an old camouflage jacket that would blend in with the hillside. There was no reason, it was just a game. The summits of the hills were powdered with snow and the sky was patched blue and white. A chill breeze blew the sea into small crested waves. As the little *Kittiwake* bounced round the headlands, I flitted from hollow to bracken-covered slope, keeping pace alongside.

After half an hour my father, who had not yet cast a line or lifted a creel, pulled into a remote inlet and jumped ashore. Hoping he would not spot me, I clambered down the grey and lichen-yellow rocks, crept closer and hid behind a boulder.

A cloud covered the sun and there was a flurry of snow, big flakes that whirled about the gully and settled on my shoulders.

My father, fifty or a hundred metres distant, stood on a rock just above the waves, facing out to sea. Believing himself unseen in that wild spot, he threw back his head and raised his arms as if he wished to fly. Then he stepped back from the brink and to my astonishment unzipped his jacket and peeled off his jersey and shirt. In less than a minute he was naked and tucked his clothes firmly into a crevice where the wind could not pluck them away. He ran his hands through his hair and lifted his arms again, exulting in the bite of the wind and sudden whip of spray against his body. Then, showing no hurt, he jumped lightly across the barnacled rocks and balanced on an outcrop just beyond the boat. Below him the waves surged and fell back in cascades, foaming about the rocks and sucking the long weed in whirlpools. In a landscape whitened by the veils of snow, my father waited for the next rising wave. As it arrived, brimming the gully, he drew back his arms and dived far out.

For two full minutes he was gone and I thought he must have drowned, then his head appeared like a seal some distance from the shore, rising on the crest of a wave and dropping into the trough beyond.

As if it were a dream I watched my father sporting, diving again and rolling and leaping in spray then swimming a long way out.

The snow passed and the March sun emerged from behind the clouds, making the sea and land sparkle.

For a while longer my father played in the crystal

water then turned and swam back to shore. Reaching the boat, he slid aboard in one sinuous movement and collected something from the bottom boards. Holding it in his teeth, he slipped back over the side.

His swimming now was more purposeful. For a long time he was gone underwater, then he rose for a breath a little way off shore and dived again. As he did so I saw that something trailed behind him. At first I could not make out what it was, but as he surfaced a second time and a third, I realized that it was a line on which were threaded several large fish. He was catching them by hand, using a bright steel hook – instead, I guessed, of those thick sharpened nails he had cut short the morning after his arrival.

The string of fish hampered his swimming. He returned to the boat and tied it to the side, then set off again.

In half an hour he had caught enough. Three lines of haddock and cod trailed from the boat's side; a few pink crabs and blue lobsters crawled about the bottom boards. Bright water cascaded from his head and shoulders as my father sprang back aboard. Briskly he pulled up the lines, secured the claws of the snapping shellfish and rinsed his fingers.

Once more ashore, he brushed the water from arms and legs with the flat of his hands and looked across the sea towards Roan Island. He was so close that I could see the yearning on his face – then suddenly a shadow of the fear that was always with him.

Reluctantly he reached for his T-shirt. Soon he was dressed and after a last look round the inlet, stepped back aboard the *Kittiwake*. Stooping to the outboard, he turned on the fuel, adjusted the choke and wrapped the starting-cord round the flywheel.

It was my last chance, I thought. My last chance to speak to my father here, alone. To tell him what I had seen. Ask what it meant. Surely he would not harm me.

He tugged the starting-cord. The engine puttered but did not fire.

I jumped from hiding and ran forward, slipping on the weedy rocks. "Dad!" The word felt strange in my mouth. "Dad!"

As if he were a startled fox, or an otter, his head jerked round. Seeing me, his arm came up as if he warded off a blow. He tried to step back, looked all about as if seeking some way of escape.

"It's all right," I called, for his alarm reached out

and touched me. "It's only me. There's no one else."

When I reached the boat neither of us knew what to say. My father sat by the engine. I stepped aboard, gripping the gunnel for balance, and sat amidships. Our eyes slid from each other. I looked out to sea. The boat rocked easily. Waves slapped against her planking.

After a long time I said, "I watched you swimming."

"Yes," he said.

"I never heard of anyone catching fish like that."

He didn't reply.

"Were you not freezing?"

With a shock I saw that he was trembling.

"It doesn't matter," I said. "I won't tell anyone."

At that his eyes turned on me. "There's things I can't tell you, Ewan. Not yet. Not ever. Terrible things."

"The night you came back," I said when he didn't continue. "You said something about dead men."

He nodded. "And more. Worse."

The boat bumped against the rocks. Staring cod

and a five-foot conger eel, killed by a deep bite across the back of the head, slithered against my shoes.

"I had to go, Ewan," my father said. "When you were little, I mean. I couldn't help it. It was..."

"It was what?" I said.

His eyes searched my face. "You blame me, don't you."

"I don't know," I said. "Nobody tells me anything."

A lock of hair discharged its load of water. He pushed it from his brow. "All right. I'll tell you so much, you need to know. For the rest – give me time. Perhaps when you're a bit older. But not all of it – never!"

I waited.

"For seven years," my father said, "I've been a prisoner. Not in jail, not tied hand and foot, but a prisoner just the same. All because of a meeting before you were born." He nodded seawards. "Out there on Roan Island. I don't know if you believe me but it's the truth."

"Roan Island!" I exclaimed. "You're not saying..."

"No, no. That's where it started. The place I was

kept prisoner was miles away, far from here. Other islands." He gestured. "Way down south near the equator."

"Are you saying you were kidnapped?"

"In a way, yes. But not like you mean."

"Well how?" I said. "Why? Who was it made you a prisoner and took you away?"

"You'll have to wait for the how and why. But who?" He shrugged simply. "Friends. People who never hurt me, people who cared for me – loved me even – just wouldn't let me go."

The word *love* hung in the air and I thought of my mother but said nothing.

"Was that where you learned to swim like this?" I said.

He took a knife from his pocket and began to clean fish scales from beneath his nails.

"We swam for our food. Most of it anyway." His brow furrowed and the haunted look returned to his eyes. "But they were warm seas, hot islands. The fish were very different from what we eat here – and there were squid, octopus, clams."

"Octopus!" I made a face. "But wasn't it dangerous? You get sharks in places like that!"

My father gave a rare smile and pulled up his

jersey. Two big moonshaped scars circled his chest and waist.

"Was that a shark?" I exclaimed.

"It was."

"What happened?"

"Oh, I was careless. Swam out beyond the reef and it went for me."

"How did you get away? Did you kill it?"

"Not me, it was enormous. But my friends were nearby, luckily. They drove it off and carried me ashore."

His mind elsewhere, my father pulled a fresh grey cod towards him and cut a wedge from its shoulder.

"Was it a great white?" I asked. "How did they drive it off?"

"You've suddenly got a lot of questions." Absently he raised the raw fish to his mouth and bit off a piece. His lips glistened. With evident enjoyment he chewed – then saw the expression on my face.

Too late he froze, hesitated about spitting his mouthful over the side, then finished chewing and swallowed.

"Well, you know that much anyway. Norwegians do it all the time."

"Eat it raw?"

"I think so. Eskimos do anyway. You should try it. It tastes better that way. Crunchy. Juicy."

The thought made me sick.

Leaning forward, my father gutted the cod which lay at his feet and threw its innards over the side. Seagulls dived, crashing into the waves and flying off with long trails hanging from their beaks. Other gulls mobbed them. Their screams filled the air.

"It's a savage world, Ewan: *nature red in tooth and claw*."

I felt my pocket. Three toffees remained. I offered them in my hand. "Would you not rather have one of these?"

He shook his head. "You eat your sweeties. And if the sight doesn't actually make you vomit, I'll – " He rinsed his fingers over the side and picked up the wedge of cod.

Now that I was prepared for it and knew that Eskimos did the same, it didn't seem so bad.

"And I'll have white teeth when you have rotten ones," my father said.

For another quarter of an hour we sat talking. Though his eyes roved constantly from the rocks to the open sea and the clear water beneath our keel, I had not seen my father so relaxed as in that wild place. Partly, I think, it was because he felt at home there; partly because there were only the two of us; and partly, perhaps, because he had unburdened himself of a little of his secret. Also I had promised not to tell my mother or anyone about the swimming.

"You're a grand lad, Ewan." He stretched out a hand and squeezed my knee. For the first time I did not recoil from him. "But we'd best be on our way or questions will be asked."

I climbed ashore and he rewound the starting cord. At the third tug the engine fired with a cloud of blue smoke and a roar that frightened a thousand seabirds from the cliffs behind us. He cast off and waved as the little *Kittiwake* puttered away down the inlet and rounded a low headland to meet the waves that rolled in from the sea. I raised a hand in reply and, wondering greatly about all that I had seen and heard, started up the steep hillside to make my way home.

## Chapter Four

# Beast on the Hill

Although I had been close to my mother all my life, I kept my word to my new-found father and did not tell her his secret. It seemed like a betrayal and I felt guilty, but a day or two later we all had something else to occupy our minds. Several things, in fact.

It started one lunchtime. I had been up the hill with Fly looking over the sheep and lambs. As I returned down the track, my mother called me from the back of the house. I went round and found her looking puzzled.

"Ewan, you haven't taken anything off the washing line?"

"No."

It was another March day of blue sky and scudding clouds. The sheets and towels and clothes fluttered bravely in a fresh wind.

"Well, those old jeans you're so fond of are missing, and your navy jersey, and a long skirt of mine."

I saw the gaps on the line and looked around.

"No, they haven't fallen or blown into a whin bush. They've just gone – and the pegs are back on the line."

"When did you put them out?"

"Yesterday afternoon, but there was that snow at teatime so I left the heavy things out overnight."

"No idea." I shrugged.

"Oh, isn't that annoying! They're not worth a lot but who on earth would come all the way down the glen here? This is the Highlands, not some tenement close in Glasgow." She sighed. "Anyway, not much we can do about it now. Come on in, lunch is about ready. How's that lamb with the bad leg?"

As it happened the lamb was progressing well. But before morning the lamb and its mother were dead, and – for the time being at least – the missing clothes were wiped from our minds.

★　★　★

The evening was cold and fair. I did my homework, telephoned a schoolfriend, carried a message to neighbours, and watched some television. At ten o'clock it was time for bed.

I was just dropping off to sleep – that point where sometimes you feel you're falling and wake with a jerk – when a distant sound penetrated my consciousness. It was not a sound I could place yet somehow it was familiar. Out on the hill some creature was screaming. It was not a dog, or the sharp call of a fox, or the bellow of a stag – they were sounds I knew. This was something else, something big, and it made my skin prickle. I sat up, listening intently, and switched on the bedside light.

There was movement downstairs. My mother's voice.

"Mum," I called loudly. "Mum! What's that noise?"

There was silence then her voice drifted up the stairs. "Just some old bull, Ewan, love. Nothing to be frightened of. Go back to sleep."

She was lying. It was no bull. Possibly a horse, for beneath the savage scream there was something of a whinny about it.

I listened a while longer then threw back my duvet. In pyjamas and barefoot, I padded down the stairs and pushed open the door of the living-room.

My mother stood by the table, straight-backed and deathly pale. My father, his eyes staring but seeing only what was in his head, sat forward in his chair.

"What is it?" I whispered. "Not the dog that came the day Dad disappeared?"

My mother said, "I don't know, Ewan."

"No. That was the black dog." My father's voice shook. "This is the horse, much worse. The white horse."

I had been right. The whinnying scream came again from the hill, closer this time.

I ran into the hall and pulled open the front door. The outside light showed no disturbance: ledges of snow lay on the peat stack, the endless wind rocked the branches of the pines.

The wild cry rang across the glen, echoing above the familiar creaks and whispers of the night. It came again, different in the open air – more clearly the scream of a horse yet reminding me somehow of a shriek of wind across the waves in a northerly storm, a savage lonely sound that made my blood run cold.

My mother joined me – and after a while, my father.

In houses across the glen other lights came on. Figures appeared in doorways.

The hillsides above us were dark and patched with snow. Clouds hid the moon. Rivers of stars showed between.

The creature, whatever it was, moved towards the sea. And now there came a new sound, the confused, terrified bleating of sheep. They were our sheep, my mother had brought them down to the pasture for lambing.

Helpless, we listened. The sound grew louder, the frantic baaing of the ewes and thinner higher strident voices of their lambs.

Then there came a distant rumbling noise. The cries of the flock rose to a crescendo.

"I can't stand it!" Pressing hands to her ears my mother ran into the house and came out thrusting cartridges into an old shotgun. "I'm going up there!"

She ran to the gate. The beam of her torch flashed wildly on whins and rocks as she started up the track.

"No!" My father ran after her. "That's half what she wants. For you to go up there!"

"I don't care!" My mother's voice was desperate. "It'll kill you!"

My mother climbed on. Then my father was at her back. He seized her anorak. "Let me go!" she cried and struck at him. Her foot slipped off the track and she tumbled. "Let me go! We were all right until you came back! I'm going up there!"

"I won't let you!" My father restrained her. "What about Ewan?"

My mother stopped then. Her face, a pale patch in the darkness, turned towards me. "But the poor sheep! The lambs!"

"I know. But there's nothing you can do. Nothing any of us can do. It's too dangerous."

My mother collapsed then, lying on the muddy track and weeping, her face pressed into the grass.

Above us, meanwhile, the screams of the white horse and baaing of the sheep continued. Their terror communicated itself to cattle and sheep throughout the glen. On all sides their lowing and bleating rose on the night.

My mother and father returned through the gate.

"But Duncan, what about our neighbours' sheep?" My mother spoke through her tears. "What about them?"

"I don't know." My father's voice was hopeless. "Now she knows I'm here, I don't know what she'll do."

At my back the telephone was ringing. Keeping her face turned from me, Mum went into the house.

"Tell them we'll go up at first light," my father called after her. "Nothing we can do right now."

But other men felt differently. Down the road torches were swaying. They approached. We heard voices. A group of six men – Magnus, old Peter and some others – turned in through our gate. Strong hands grasped sticks and garden forks. Magnus saw the shotgun beneath my father's arm.

"Good man. You're with us, then. Whatever it is up there, a couple of barrels of that'll put a stop to it."

My father opened his mouth to refuse, then saw me watching. The others were watching too.

"Right." It was all he could say.

"Come on, then. Got a torch?"

Reluctantly he took it from my mother, who had come back out, and they started up the track.

"Can I go, Mum?"

"What! Absolutely not. Anyway, what are you doing out here in the middle of the night in your pyjamas? And barefoot! You'll catch your death of cold. Come on, back into the house."

But we both stood watching as the torches of the men wound through bushes and vanished into a hollow of the hill.

Higher up, in the pasture, the panic and confusion seemed to be less. The bleats were fewer, the screams of the white horse – if that's what it was – were less frequent.

Then we went indoors.

"Straight back to bed, Ewan," my mother said briskly. "Shall I bring you a hot-bottle?"

"No, I'm not cold at all." I pretended to yawn. "Sleepy, though."

"Well, no nightmares." Her hands and jacket were muddy, her eyes red from crying. "Whatever it is up there, you'll find out in the morning." She gave me a kiss and I went back upstairs.

But I didn't sleep. Sitting on the bed, I listened as my mother washed and changed. The living-room door shut and I heard a rattle of the poker as she stirred the peats. Then I pulled on my new jeans, dark jersey and anorak, pushed my feet into trainers, tiptoed downstairs and let myself from the house.

I knew the hill as well as I knew my own bedroom.

With all those men up there, I reasoned, there would be little danger for me.

My eyes soon accustomed themselves to the dark. In any case, the clouds were opening and every few minutes the moon appeared.

The blood-chilling noises from the hill had ceased, and as I limped up the track I realized that a strange silence had fallen over the glen. No rabbits rustled in the winter grasses; no bird flapped away with cries of alarm. It was eerie. Unceasingly, as I climbed towards the pasture, I scanned the shadows to left and right and looked back over my shoulder.

Then, a short distance ahead, I heard the voices of the men. One of them spotted me or heard my footfall.

"Who's that?" His voice was sharp.

"Ewan," I called at once.

"What, my Ewan?" This was my father's voice. "Where?"

"Here." I climbed the gate in the drystone dyke.

"You should be in bed! There'll be hot trouble when you go back." He put an arm round my shoulders. "Still, you'd better stay now you're here."

"Has the beast-thing gone?"

"Seems like it," old Peter said.

"What about the sheep?"

"Bad news, boy. Bad news."

Then I saw them, some pale in the darkness, others glimpsed in the beams of torches. All that I could see were dead, some torn and bloody.

"The whole flock?"

Magnus nodded. "'Fraid so, Ewan."

The ewes that my mother and I had cared for year after year, fed in the snow, seen through lambing. I ran a short way across the pasture and looked around.

"But this is only a few of them. Where are the rest?"

"It kicked the dyke down," old Peter said.

Another man pointed.

I ran down the slope to the wall above the sea, the most carefully maintained of all on our croft and topped with two strands of wire. Near one corner the stones had been tumbled, leaving a gap. Just beyond was a tremendous cliff where all day the seabirds wheeled and circled. Fragments of wool clung to the fallen rocks. Through this gap the white horse – whatever kind of beast it was – had driven our flock. In my mind's eye I saw their terror as they crushed together, struggling to escape through the gap; saw the creature with its tossing mane and rolling eye, biting with its red teeth, slashing with its sharp hooves.

My father joined me, shining his torch on the edge of the precipice. Torn grass and dislodged stones showed where the poor sheep and lambs, checking too late, had skidded over into space. I shuddered, imagining the fall, their woolly coats dashed on the sea rocks below. Though I peered down from the very brink, all was dark and I could make out nothing but the white surge of the waves. I knew how they would look, for I had seen occasional dead sheep on the rocks before, broken and mag-gotty, or tumbled by the foam and sucked away, bumping and rolling into the deep water beyond.

Suddenly, above the whine of the wind and soft roar of the sea, I thought I heard a new sound. Laughter. Surely I was mistaken. I listened intently and it came again. There was no doubt – a woman's laughter. Musical and clear, though soft, it rose from the darkness beneath me. My skin tingled. I had never heard a sound so beautiful or so cruel in my life.

The men who were with us, standing back in the

pasture, heard nothing, but a look of terror came over my father's face.

"No!" he roared. "No!"

Dropping the torch, which bounced down the grass and vanished over the precipice, he clapped both hands over his ears and stumbled back across the fallen dyke.

"Never! No! Leave me alone!"

His foot skidded and he fell full length. Even then, so great was his fear of that mysterious laughter that his hands remained clamped to his head. Scrambling to his feet, he ran the full length of the pasture. The other men, astonished, shone their torches on him as he passed. I was embarrassed and ashamed. Frantically he clambered over the gate at the top, and the last I saw of my father at that time was his back, lurching down through the whins towards home.

The moon emerged from behind a filmy cloud. Magnus, Peter and the others drew together, glancing towards me. I did not join them.

A single sheep, its eye staring and fleece bloody, lay dead at the gap in the dyke. I looked back at the sea. No sound rose above the crag but the soft incessant roar of the waves and the cry of a restless gull.

# Chapter Five

# The Boy on the Beach

News of the events that night spread rapidly and our glen was invaded. Reporters descended with notebooks; radio journalists thrust microphones at us; sightseers with video cameras roamed the cliffs and seashore. Even though none of us had actually seen the beast, for two days we were famous. But I told nobody about the laughter. And my father, whose behaviour had been the subject of much speculation, refused to leave the house or speak to any reporter. With no fresh news or further incident their interest waned. Long before a week was up the last visitor had departed and the glen returned to its customary way of life.

A second outcome of that savage night was that I

began to carry a knife for protection. It was my mother's suggestion; my mother, the most peace-loving of women. "The day your father disappeared," she said, "you were attacked by the black dog. Now he's come back and we've got the white horse. The glen's become a dangerous place for our family. I'll ferry you to the school bus, but you can't stay indoors all the time. A knife's not much, but if the worst comes to the worst, it might give you some protection." And so, like my Highland ancestors with their dirks for hunting and fighting, I slid a horn-handled sheath knife on to the belt of my jeans.

A photograph, which appeared in several newspapers, showed me heaving the dead sheep which lay in the pasture into a heap for collection by the knacker's lorry. I had gone up with Magnus, for my mother, normally so determined, could not bear it. Ever since my father's disappearance she had tended and improved the flock – hauling feed through the snow, sleepless at lambing time, tramping far across the hills in storm and sunshine – and now not a single ewe or lamb remained. It was a disaster, the loss of everything she had worked for. No matter how we tried to keep our spirits up, for the next few days the house, normally so cheerful, was pervaded with gloom.

One evening, with Fly trotting around me, I walked down to the shore. The days were lengthening and I thought I would see what had been washed up by some recent spring tides.

It was peaceful on the beach, the sea turning silver, waves breaking on the bright sand. Among the familiar tangle of weed and shells I found a few objects worth collecting: two clean planks, an orange fishing buoy, a netting needle, a twenty-metre straggle of new rope. I coiled it up and made a pile at the head of the beach then wandered on, every so often glancing behind and scanning the dunes for danger.

There are two sandy bays and as I clambered round the rocks into the second and less visited, I was surprised to see a boy playing in the stream that runs down the beach from the hillside. I was surprised because this was a boy I did not know and it was not the tourist season. He looked up and saw me. I waved, jumped down to the sand and crossed to talk to him.

Clearly he spent much of his time in the open air, for his face was fresh and his eyes sparkled. Long hair, dark as my own, hung to his shoulders. He wore a jersey and old jeans wet to the knee. I found out that he was nearly fifteen, three years older than myself.

"Hello."

"Hello."

We stood regarding each other, neither knowing quite what to say.

"Damming the stream?"

"Yes."

I looked round for Fly but she was nowhere to be seen. "Fly?" I called loudly. "Fly!" But she did not appear. It was unlike her to run off, she enjoyed our trips to the shore. Had I been more alert her disappearance might have put me on my guard. As it was I took little notice, she knew the shore even better than I did, and I turned back to the boy in the stream.

The pool he was making was sweet and fresh, but like all our water, tinted a light beer-brown by the peat. I scooped up a handful of moist sand to close a breach where the water was breaking through.

"Do you live round here?" I asked, knowing the answer.

"Not close." He looked right and left and

gestured vaguely along the coast. "Over that way."

"Where?"

"Oh, it's a small place, you wouldn't know it. What about you?"

"Just up the glen there."

Barefoot, he splashed to the far side of the pool where the dam was breaking down again. As he did so I spotted a paint streak on the leg of his jeans. My old ones had a mark just the same. In fact, they *were* my jeans; the torn back pocket, the frayed ankles where my mother had unpicked the seams. It was the pair that had vanished off the washing line, a bit tight and several centimetres short on the older boy. It was my jersey too. I looked round for his shoes and socks or a jacket but could not see any.

After all that had happened my instinct was to run. Instead I pretended not to notice. "How did you get down here? I didn't see you on the road."

"Same as anyone else." He shrugged. "You can't have been looking. What a lot of questions."

I was sure there had been no car. Anyway, who had been driving? He was lying, a thief. Yet despite this I felt easy with him, not at all threatened. Kicking off my shoes and tugging up the legs of my jeans, I joined him in the pool. Together we strengthened the dam and broadened it. Little by little the pool deepened.

Accidentally I splashed him. Scooping water in his hands and laughing, he splashed me back.

Then I saw his fingernails.

Like my father's had been, only more so, they were thick and pointed, real claws. I froze, staring. He saw my sudden change and looked down. Loosely curling his fingers into fists, he hid his nails. It was too late.

I gripped the knife at my waist. "Who are you? Wearing my clothes, lying about where you come from."

"I'm –" He opened his arms in a gesture of peace and stepped towards me.

"Keep away!" I retreated and drew my bright blade from its sheath.

He stopped then, still in the water. "I know who you are. Your name's Ewan – Ewan McKenzie. I've been waiting for you."

"Why?" I glanced round the beach.

"Because –" He hesitated to say it. "Because you're my brother."

The words struck me into confusion. I had no brother.

"Your –" I searched for his meaning. "What are you talking about? How can you be my brother?"

"Truly." He nodded, his eyes earnest, and stepped out of the pool.

I stared at him.

"Don't you see we're alike?"

He was right. We were alike. The same black hair, my father's unusual eyes.

"Only we have different mothers. Your mother, her name is Jessie. She lives up the glen." He pointed back the way I had come. "My mother's different. Her name is Neiraa. But you and I, we have the same father."

I did not know what to say and sat down on the sand. The brimming pool broke through the dam and began to drain away.

He sat beside me and toyed with a shell. "I'm not like you, though. I'm what your people might call a sea boy. Have you heard of us? Heard of our silver belts?"

I had indeed. The superstitious old folk were always telling stories of the mermaids and seal people which at one time inhabited our coast.

"Well." He felt in a tight pocket and pulled out a shimmering strip of cloth or skin. It was very fine and covered all over with scales like a fish or a snake. In breadth it was about three centimetres and at the end was a buckle of green shell. "Most of the time I live in the sea, but sometimes I want to come on land. If I take off this belt I become a boy like you."

I put out my hand to examine the belt but he snatched it back. "No, it's too precious. If I lose my belt I can never return to the sea. Then I'd pine away and die. I wouldn't be the first, it's happened to many sea boys: Meraid, Tang, the great Vraka. Our legends are full of them."

He allowed me to feel just an end of the belt. It was supple, smooth, warm.

"Put it on," I said.

"In a while," he said. "Before I leave."

"I don't know your name."

"Apsu," he said. "Some call me 'the gentle one'."

"Why?"

"Because my people are fierce." He spread his fingers. "The others have longer nails than these – for catching food and fighting. And their jaws are strong. They're hunters and do things that," he hesitated and a smile and shadow chased each other across his face, "that it's better you don't know about."

"Terrible things?" I said. "Cruel things?"

"To you, perhaps. To me –? We're hunters, it's how we live."

I thought about this, and things my father had said, and how he had come home half mad. Apsu was right, I didn't want to know any more.

I changed the subject. "Is it true that your girls are so beautiful? Do they really sit on rocks combing their hair?"

He smiled. "Yes, sometimes – on rocks or soft grass above the shore. But it's not only the girls who are beautiful. People say my mother's the most beautiful of all."

"And when sailors hear their singing," I thought of the laughter I had heard above the cliff, "does it drive them mad? Do they sail their ships on to the rocks to reach the shore?"

"I don't know if they go mad," said Apsu, "but it's true, men can't resist. The singing enchants them. And when they see how beautiful our girls are they run their boats into the surf and wreck them."

"And then the girls rescue them," I said.

He didn't reply.

"You don't mean they're drowned!" I exclaimed. "You don't let them drown!"

Apsu turned the seashell and explored its opening with a nail.

"Have you got any other powers?" I said after a while, trying not to think of poor drowning sailors. "Your people, I mean."

"More than humans?" he said. "What *you* might call magic or supernatural?"

"I suppose so."

Apsu thought. "We can summon up storms," he said, "turn a calm sea into a tumult, or make the wind drop and the waves die down again. But it's tiring, we don't do it often."

"Could you do it now?"

"I'm half human, remember," he said. "I'm not so good at it. Besides," he glanced down at his legs, "I've taken off my silver belt."

"Try," I said.

He smiled again, then pushed the hair from his eyes and looked out to sea. His brow wrinkled with concentration.

After a moment I was surprised to feel a wind on my face – and was it my imagination or had the clouds darkened? Then a rougher wave than previously rolled in from the sea and crashed about the rocks. It was followed by another.

Apsu relaxed, his brow smoothed. The wind ceased and the bright water cascaded from rock pools.

"That's fantastic!" I said.

He lay on the sand and then, forgetting perhaps that he wore clothes, rolled down into what remained of the pool. It was about thirty centimetres deep. He shook his head in the water and came up streaming.

"I've told you something about how we live." Lying on his stomach, propped on elbows, he looked up at me from the beer-brown pool. "Tell me about land people, about yourself."

Shivering to see him and feeling the evening grow colder, I zipped my jacket to the throat and told him about my life in the glen, and my mother, and school, and my father's return.

Apsu had many questions but at length all was said and we fell silent.

The tide had been rising all the while and now the white rim of the waves reached almost to where we lay.

Apsu rose in the rippling pool and stripped off his jersey – my jersey.

"Ah!" He stretched bare arms to the breeze. "That feels better."

Then he hung the silver belt around his neck and tugged off the sodden jeans. Naked as bathtime, he stood on the darkening beach and buckled the shimmering strip around his waist. And in an instant, so fast that I never saw the change, it was not a boy like myself who stood before me, but a sea boy whose waist merged into a long beautiful tail which splashed in the freshwater pool.

I stared, amazed and delighted. Apsu, my half-brother – strangely, I could now think of him as that – smiled up at me.

The waves reached the dam and soon its disintegration was complete.

"Now I must go back to the sea," said Apsu. On hands and tail, like a seal, he lolloped down the shining sand.

I went with him, ignoring the rush and hiss of waves that broke over my feet.

"And I have to go home," I said. "Fly'll have run back ages ago. After what happened the other night, Mum'll be worried."

"The white horse." Apsu's face grew serious. "I tried to persuade Myami – my mother – not to send it but she wouldn't listen. It had to be."

"Why?" I exclaimed angrily. "Why did it have to be? Why did she want to kill all our sheep? Mum and I have looked after them for years. The wool and the lambs – they're our livelihood."

"But you must know why." Apsu was surprised.

"No."

"Well, why do you think we are here? To take my father home again."

"Home!" I said. "But he's my father too."

"Then come with us." He thought about it. "It would be good. I'd like that."

"But what about my mother?"

"He was married to my mother first! I'm older than you."

"Has he been living with you all this time?"

He nodded. "For the last seven years."

A big wave swept in, surging to my knees. Apsu flipped his tail and spray cascaded about our heads. The wave retreated.

"So when I was little," I said, "did she come back and take him away with her? The day he disappeared and everyone thought he had drowned, is that what happened?"

"You must know it is."

"And did she send the black dog," I said, "like she sent the white horse? The black dog that did this to my leg," I pulled my jeans higher to show him the scars, "and disfigured my mother's face?"

"She was very pretty, your mother," Apsu said. "And you were the image of our father, a handsome young boy. My mother, she was jealous. So she took her husband away and sent the black dog to deal with you."

"To deal with me?" I cried. "To kill me? If Mum hadn't been so brave it would have torn me apart!"

"That's what I meant." Apsu was unabashed. "As I told you, we're sea people, not like you. We're hunters, that's why we have claws. Think of your tiger. Think of the orca."

As he was speaking I spotted a swirl in the water by some sheltered rocks. It calmed. I was still staring at the spot when from out of the waves, only a few metres distant, the head and shoulders of a woman emerged.

I have never seen anything more beautiful than Neiraa appeared at that moment. A necklace of pink shells was about her throat, strands of weed were twisted round her brow, her long hair floated in the waves. Framed by these, her features were perfect, her eyes so clear and free and wild that I have no power to describe them.

"I felt you raise the waters, Apsu," she said. "So I came." Her eyes turned on me. "I have no need to ask who this is."

I felt powerless, listening to her voice, staring as the waves washed about her shoulders and her long tail curled in the sea.

"Ewan McKenzie," she said. "You are so like my Apsu. Come, let me see you more closely." She stretched out a hand.

And I would have gone, had not three things happened at almost the same moment:

Apsu cried, "No, Myami! You mustn't!"

I saw her dagger-like nails, so different from her smile.

And my mother's voice, calling "Ewan! Ew-a-a-an!" reached me round the headland.

In a daze, as if waking from a dream, I regained my senses and stepped back from the water's edge. A sudden flash of fury transformed Neiraa's lovely face. In an instant it was gone.

"Come then, Apsu. Say goodbye to your brother. Or perhaps you can persuade him to come with us to the islands. With his father."

"I've already invited him."

As a wave lifted him from the sand, he swept his tail once and arrowed out to his mother's side.

"Goodbye, Ewan." He raised a hand. "We'll meet again soon, I promise."

"And be sure to tell your father of our meeting," called Neiraa.

At the sound of even those few words I felt myself slipping back towards a dream and pinched the back of my leg hard.

"Ew-a-a-an!" My mother's voice was nearer.

"Here," I called loudly. "Coming."

Then my brother and his mother, Apsu and Neiraa, swam out through the breaking waves. Briefly I saw their heads beyond. With a flip, like dolphins, they dived and were gone from sight.

For a full minute I stood watching. Apsu's discarded jeans and jersey tumbled up the beach and lay stranded as the waves retreated. I rescued them and rinsed out the sand, then started across the beach to meet my mother, whose white Arran jumper caught the last of the daylight beneath the darkening cliff.

## Chapter Six

# Flight from the Enchantress

"Yes," my father said. "It's perfectly true. Apsu's your brother. I just didn't know how to tell you."

"Does Mum know?"

He nodded.

"And is Neiraa your wife? Were you married to her before you married Mum?"

"Not the way we think of it," said my father. "Anyway, she'd gone back to the sea, disappeared, been gone for a couple of years. Let me try to explain, tell you what happened."

We sat in the barn, I on the sweet-smelling hay, my father on an old trestle by the wall. Birds flitted through the small window, building nests on the ledges.

"I was little more than a lad then," he leaned forward, "nineteen or so with my own boat, fishing out by Roan Island. It was a hot day and I'd put ashore for a cool dip and my sandwiches. Nobody goes to the island – hardly ever, anyway, three miles out – and I was lying there on the beach, half asleep in the sun, when what do I see but this girl with a long fish's tail coming up out of the waves. It was Neiraa, about the same age as myself. She'd been watching me fishing. Anyway, she took off the silver belt and wrapped a piece of cloth around her like a sarong. I'd never seen anything so beautiful in my life."

He stared into space, remembering.

"I think I must have been enchanted – they can, you know. It was June when we first met and we went on meeting all that long summer. Out on the island. When I look back on it now it's all a bit of a daze.

"Then it was September and the weather grew colder, north winds and rain. And one morning when I sailed out to the island she just wasn't there. I was devastated. I waited all day – and went again the next morning – and the next – but she never came back."

"Why?" I said.

"Well, I was only a young fisherman. At the time I thought maybe she'd had an accident, or just got tired of me and gone off. Later I found out that she'd realized she was expecting Apsu and wanted to be with her own people."

I thought about it. "And then you met Mum?"

"A year or so later, yes."

"And forgot all about Neiraa?"

"Well no, not forgot. You never forget. But as I said, it was like a dream, gone with that whole summer. And now your mother and I, ordinary young people, were very much in love. We married, you came along, life seemed perfect."

"Then she came back."

"After seven years."

"And wanted you to go away with her – to those far-off islands."

He nodded. "I told her *no* and she was angry. Told me about Apsu. Made terrible threats towards you and your mother. I told her I was just a man, she was a sea maid. She should find one of her own kind."

My father's eyes slid from my face.

"But then she used her powers to enchant me

again. I was down at the shore, just cast off in the boat. She was more beautiful than ever. She smiled, she sang. I felt my senses slipping away. Then the white horses came – not hurting me, you understand, just galloping in the waves – and a gale began to blow from the land. Before I knew it we were far out at sea. Neiraa was ecstatic. And so was I, I couldn't help it. But every so often, just for a few seconds, the veil parted and I remembered everything I was leaving behind. I raged. I shouted. My life was here with you and your mother! I had to go back!"

"She stopped you?"

"Without her help there was no way I could get back. And Neiraa loved me. She'd never stopped loving me. As she saw it, I was *her* husband, the father of Apsu. And little by little, with her smiles and magic, every memory of my human life was washed away – like that dam of yours in the sand. Everything was new-born: the sea, the sun, the tropical islands we sailed to, Neiraa herself and our little sea boy."

"And you never thought about Mum and me?"

"Not for a long time. I've just told you, all my past life was wiped from my mind."

"Like Circe and Odysseus," I said.

"What?"

"This book we read in school."

"I know nothing about that," my father said.

"Were you happy there?"

"At the beginning, yes. It was all a great adventure. There were no worries, no work. The sea gave us fish to eat, the bushes were full of fruit. I learned to swim and dive."

"It sounds wonderful," I said.

"It was for a long time – weeks, years, I don't remember. We played on the sands and in the lagoon; games with pearls and fabulous shells and treasures the sea washed up. At night the air smelled of blossom and the ocean."

He fell silent.

"But it wasn't always like that?"

"No. It wasn't. Sitting here it's hard to believe any of it really happened. But it did."

As if to reassure himself he pulled up his jersey and surveyed the terrible shark bite. It was not his only scar. I had seen other wounds, long healed, on his legs and shoulders.

"These sea people," I said, "were they the friends you talked about who rescued you from the shark?"

"And a giant octopus too. But that was part of the good times."

"So did something happen? What made it change?"

"I don't know exactly, I just began to feel different – an outsider." A haunted look came into my father's eyes. "Then there were the bad things." His lips trembled. "It wasn't a dream any more – it was a nightmare."

Fly, who lay on the hay beside me, gave a whine. I patted her shoulder reassuringly.

"What bad things?" I said.

He looked at me. I hope when I grow older I never have such terrible memories.

"Apsu said it was better I didn't know," I said.

"He was right."

"But just tell me a little," I said. "So I understand."

My father struggled with the words. "Singing the boats ashore," he whispered. "Typhoons and shipwrecks. Sea maids laughing and pointing and dancing while the sailors drowned. Diving into the white waves and dragging bodies ashore. Treasures from the ships. Then feasting." He covered his eyes. "And later, when the sun and salt water had finished bleaching, games with the skulls of the dead sailors along the beach. Underwater gardens made of bones. Skeletons hanging like mobiles from the palm trees, clicking in the wind."

His shoulders shook and I saw that he was crying. I crossed the barn and crouched beside him and put an arm round his shoulders.

"Sorry, Ewan." He looked at me with a tear-stained face and rubbed his cheeks with a hand.

"That's OK," I said, though shaken to see my father so broken.

Slowly he calmed and gave me a hug that made my joints crack.

I threw some armfuls of hay on the floor beside him and sat on it.

"Seven years." His voice still shook. "Towards the end I was sure I would go mad. Until one day, at the far side of the outermost island, I saw a ship. It was a hilly island with trees. The afternoon was hot and still so almost everyone, including the lookout, was sleeping in the shade, or on smooth rocks and in the shallows about the great lagoon. Carefully, with the piece of glass I wore among the shells and little trinkets round my neck, I lit a smoky fire and set out swimming from the shore.

Whatever happened, I no longer cared, I had to get away. Even if a tiger shark got me, at least it would be quick.

"Some people might not understand: Neiraa was more beautiful than ever, Apsu was a fine son, the islands were wonderful. But if I stayed there any longer, I was sure I would die.

"Luck was with me. The lookout on the bridge of the ship saw the smoke and it altered course. You see, the islands aren't marked on any map. If a ship sails close enough the sea people lure it on to the reef. The coast's littered with wrecks.

"I was over a mile out before I was spotted, waving a dried-out palm branch I had towed behind me. At the same time, back on the island, the sea people saw my smoke signal and I was missed by Neiraa. Then the lookout saw the ship – and my palm branch.

"They went wild. Immediately Neiraa and a dozen others set out to bring me back. The rest gathered along the shore and began the singing that drives men from their senses.

"It was a close thing. The engines of the great ship were stopped and it drifted alongside me, towering overhead. At the same time the sea people, lashing their tails and hissing with fury, swam in as fast as dolphins from the other direction. The sailors saw them, pointing and laughing, but the pilot ladder was ready and they bundled it over the rail, rattling down the ship's side. Desperately I swam up, caught hold of it and hauled myself from the water. The next second the sea people were at my heels, clawing with their long nails, leaping out of the calm sea to drag me back. Luckily I was just beyond their reach and scrambled up the long ladder to the deck.

"It wasn't a cruise ship but it did carry a few passengers. I think everyone was astonished, especially the ladies, to see a naked man come aboard from the sea. I must have looked three-quarters mad: brown and scarred, weed woven through my hair, a ragged beard, and a fantastical necklace round my throat.

"But the figures who had pursued me were stranger still. Looking down, I saw them circling, beautiful and silver-tailed. The water was so clear, like blue-green crystal. And now the sea people looked up with smiles, waving and calling, for the ship was a great prize. A mile away the palm-fringed islands stood between sea and sky. Across the waves drifted the sound of singing – I could tell from the faces of the crew.

"A sailor brought me a pair of old shorts and I put them on. The captain came down from the bridge. I ran across and grabbed his arm. 'Captain!' I cried. 'Captain! Start the engines! Sail away from here! Quick or it'll be too late!' But it was too late already. He had listened to the voices, his eyes had that faraway look I had seen so often.

"My own ears were still blocked with seawater. Before they could clear, I snatched a wad of cotton waste from the back pocket of one of the sailors, pulled off a scrap and plugged them tight.

"The man scarcely noticed. I looked around me. The other sailors were the same. Jostling for the best position, they gathered along the rails, all waving and calling down, looking towards the islands. A pair of binoculars went from hand to hand. They cupped their ears to hear more clearly.

" 'Don't!' I tugged their shirts. 'Don't listen!'

"But no one paid any attention.

" 'Half ahead, both engines!' the captain called up to the bridge.

" 'Half ahead both,' replied the officer on watch.

"I heard the ring of the controls, then beneath my feet the slow throb and vibration of the engines.

" 'Steer for the shore.'

" 'Aye-aye, sir.'

"The big ship swung. Directly ahead lay the coral reef and sharp fangs of rock. Day and night the sea surged white around them. At my back I felt the wind freshen. The sea people were working their magic.

" 'No!' I seized the captain's collar. 'Turn back! Turn back!'

"He pushed me away.

"All eyes, eager, sparkling, were now fixed on the islands and the bright waves beneath us. To port and starboard the sea people were beckoning, laughing, leaping and diving like porpoises. The sailors' teeth showed in excited smiles. How often I had seen similar teeth grinning from skulls as we threw them along the sands.

"Neiraa, the most lovely of all, looked up and caught my eye.

"The wind strengthened. The waves mounted.

"What could I do? In the water the sea people would be upon me in seconds. The sailors, helpless as moths in a candle flame, went to their fate. Surely there was some way I could save them. I looked around. How could I deaden their ears to that enchanted singing?

"The answer came in a flash. I looked up at the black and orange funnel. There, at the top of a narrow iron ladder, was the ship's siren. Running, I climbed from deck to deck, past the bridge, past the lifeboats, and mounted the ladder. In a minute I was there. The foaming reef drew closer. Hastily, for I didn't want to be deafened, I pulled the cotton waste from the pocket of my shorts and plugged my ears tighter. Then I tugged the wire cable that worked the siren.

"At once an ear-splitting *bo-o-o-om* resounded across the sea. *Bo-o-o-o-om*!

"Steam spouted above my head. Scalding drops of water spattered my shoulders.

"I pulled the cable again and didn't let go. Angry faces stared up from the deck. Two sailors ran through the ship and began to climb the narrow ladder. The noise of the siren hurt their ears. I kicked them back with my bare feet.

"From such a height the sea people were small and wonderfully graceful. They realized what I was doing, even though the sailors didn't. It was rarely a ship of that size came close to the islands; I was depriving them of a great celebration. Their beckoning grew desperate. Several pointed at me and made threatening gestures. Smiles were replaced by snarls.

"*Bo-o-o-o-om!* The sound of the siren never ceased.

"Second by second the waves were building up. Foam and white horses galloped on the crests. From the island a hundred more sea people slipped into the water and swam out towards us through the boiling reef.

"Meanwhile, on the ship, the sailors rubbed their eyes and blinked about them. The enchantment of the sea people was broken.

"The captain, perhaps because he was the oldest, was among the first. The great ship and all its crew and passengers were in his charge. Directly ahead lay the coral reef.

" 'Full astern both!' he roared up at the bridge, but the officer on watch did not respond.

"I guessed what the captain was shouting and released the siren for a moment. A sudden, startling peace fell over the sea.

" 'Full astern both!'

" 'Aye-aye, sir.'

"I tugged on the siren again. Beneath me the whole vessel shuddered as the engines went into full reverse. The twin propellers churned the water but still the ship slid forward – it takes a long time to stop a vessel of 20,000 tons. The sea was a turmoil. The reef came closer and closer. It seemed impossible we wouldn't go aground. Sailors ran to the bow and leaned over the sides, clothes and hair tossed by the gale that blew from astern, driving the ship forward. Below them in the crashing water the sea people waited, eager for the moment of impact, fearful they would be deprived of it. Only Neiraa, among those savage faces, remained calm, smiling up from the storm, as irresistibly beautiful as ever. For a moment I faltered, the siren cable fell slack in my hand, then I shut my eyes tight and tugged again.

"The bow of the ship just touched – there was damage when we reached port – then the tremendous engines began to pull us back. The sailors cheered, now trading shouts and curses with the figures in the water. The captain returned to the bridge and all the crew were ordered indoors. Spray was exploding mast-high and waves broke clear across the deck.

"Slowly the great ship retreated, turned, and began to draw away. One mile of stormy water, then two, separated us from the islands. As the last of the sea people slipped astern, I released the siren.

"The sudden silence clapped about my ears. Then I became aware of the full force of the gale. In all my time on the islands I had never known a storm so wild. The wind battered about me, blowing the flags stiff and flinging the funnel smoke astern. The ship rolled so heavily that one moment the leaping sea was beneath me to port, the next to starboard. Clinging tight, I descended the ladder and two of the crew helped me to safety.

"For several days, despite the earplugs, I was quite deaf. Most of the time I was unaware because the captain kept me sedated. I didn't just look three-quarters mad, I really was, and scalded about the back and shoulders.

"Still, I was alive and free. We all were. To the passengers and some of the sailors I was a hero. Once I'd recovered a bit they used to come and sit with me in the cabin or out on deck. But a lot of the crew were resentful; they couldn't get the picture of those beautiful girls out of their minds.

"The captain wanted a full report for his log.

He'd seen the sea people and he was a kind man, but most of the time I lied. Who I was, where I came from, how I came to be on the islands, how we lived there – I couldn't bear to talk about it.

"When we reached port in South America, it was even worse. The ship was besieged by officials in uniform and reporters who wanted the story. They wouldn't leave me alone. In the end I had to lock myself in my cabin, barricade the door and shut the porthole curtains to get away from them.

"That night I fled the ship. There was a watchman on the gangway, so I let myself over the side and swam ashore. Slowly I worked my way up to the Panama Canal and stowed away on a ship bound for Liverpool.

"The rest you know."

As my father finished, he sank back against the rough wall of the barn. He was exhausted, his face drained of colour.

For a minute neither of us spoke. The only sounds were those of the glen: the breeze, the distant sea and the fluttering of birds.

"But I don't know everything," I said. "Did she tell you nothing about the black dog which –" I touched my knee – "and scarred Mum's face?"

"Not a word. It never occurred to me. It's very rare for the sea people to use the black dogs." He put out a hand. "I'm so sorry, Ewan."

"And the white horse?"

"Ah, that's different. The white horse and the sea people, they swim together. Both can go on sea and land. The sea people ride them. But they're not like the horses we know, these horses eat flesh and fish, crunch up lobsters. Neiraa sent the white horse to drive your mother's sheep over the cliff."

"Why?"

"Didn't Apsu tell you? Because she hates her. She's jealous. She knows I love your mother, a good love. Your mother's not like her, she's beautiful inside as well as out. Neiraa wants to destroy her but doesn't know how. Not yet."

"Can't you stop her?"

"Give you and your mother some protection? Of course. I only have to walk down to the beach. Let her take me back to the islands. She loves me, heaven help me. I don't know any other way."

"But Mum loves you too," I said. "And there's me."

"I know," he said. "Do you think I don't realize? Do you think I don't care? But what should I do? It's

83

the devil or the deep blue sea. If I go, we'll never see each other again. There won't be another ship. And if I stay, goodness knows what she'll do."

I thought about it. "Whether you go or not," I said, "she might send the black dog again, or something worse. So you should stay."

He didn't reply.

"I have seen her," I said after a minute. "When I was with Apsu. I told you. She must be the most beautiful woman in the world."

He nodded. "And the most pitiless."

I stood and picked stalks of hay from my jersey. Twelve years old, what could I say? But my father's words reminded me of something.

"You said they were tropical islands. And Neiraa went away when it got cold here in September. But you swam naked in the sea in March. It was freezing!"

"I can't tell you everything," he said, "not in half an hour. I was there for seven years, remember. We made journeys. I got used to the cold. If you go back in time, men didn't always have jackets and trousers. To tell you the truth," he plucked at his jersey, "I don't feel comfortable wearing these things now."

I looked at him and suddenly we both burst out laughing.

"You're right," he said. "If we didn't, we'd see some funny sights."

"Mrs McPhee!" I said.

"Stop it!" he said. "You'll put me off my tea."

And together, with Fly scampering ahead, we walked from the barn into the spring sunshine.

I was glad to have my father home and I didn't want him to go away again.

# Chapter Seven

# 2 a.m.

I don't know if it was the singing that woke me or
my father shouting downstairs. Drowsily I lay
listening then sat up and switched on the bedside
lamp. My eyes stabbed and I had to pick up the
clock. It was two o'clock in the morning.

After my father's warning about revenge we had
been expecting the singing and each night I left two
tufts of cottonwool beside the bed to plug my
ears. Quickly I reached for them and stuffed one
into my left ear, but before I did the right I paused
for a moment to listen, so that I would know and
remember what this enchanted singing sounded
like. Just for a second, I thought – but that second
was too long. The melody and the voice drifting

through the night were so lovely, so innocent, that I realized my father was wrong. There was no danger. I removed the cottonwool from my left ear to hear more clearly.

Downstairs, meanwhile, my father – for my mother still made him sleep on the settee – was raging and shouting. His ears, I realized, must be covered, and I wished he would be quiet for his noise disturbed the magic of the night. My mother had gone down to him. I heard her soothing voice and the chink of a bottle as she poured him a glass of whisky.

They irritated me and I wanted to be out of doors so that I could hear the singing better still. Best of all, I could run down to the shore and meet the beautiful woman who I knew was waiting for me by the sea. The beams of a bright moon shone through my bedroom window.

It only took a minute to dress and thrust a bundle of clothes beneath the duvet to look as if I was still sleeping. Then I opened my bedroom door and crept quietly downstairs.

"... stay here with you and Ewan," I heard my father sob as I crossed the hall. "... won't ever give up ... wants me back and means to have me!"

"Ssshhh! Duncan!" I heard my mother's comforting words. "You're safe here. It's all right."

Perhaps my mother, being a woman, couldn't hear the singing. Perhaps it was directed only at my father and me. I didn't stop to think about it. I didn't care. My only interest was to escape from the house.

Because of recent events, the door was now locked at night. I turned the key and slipped out, softly pulled the door shut behind me, and ran through grass to the gate. Pausing beneath the pine trees, I remembered that as well as the cottonwool, I had placed some other items on the bedside table to protect me: the sheath-knife, some sharp pebbles, a toy car with a pointed end. Some time previously I had seen a film in which a secret agent pressed an iron nail into the palm of his hand so that the pain would stop him from being brainwashed; I had thought the pointed car might do the same if Neiraa started singing. The pebbles were to drop into my shoes so that the discomfort might have the same effect. I had forgotten them and now they seemed silly, childish ideas. Why should I need protecting? This was the most exciting thing that had ever happened to me.

I hurried on. Though two other croft houses were as close to the shore as ours, no lights were showing and the road was deserted except for an occasional sheep. The sky was almost cloudless. The moon, three-quarters full, lit the surrounding fields and white rim of the waves as they broke on the beach. On all sides, accompanied by the murmur of the sea, the soft singing of Neiraa filled the air. I could not wait to reach the shore and broke into a run.

The road turned left to the harbour but the beach lay straight ahead. Plunging round tussocks of grass, I descended the dunes to the white sand.

A hundred metres distant, perfectly still, a figure stood above the ebbing tide. What I had expected, I don't know: Neiraa with her shining tail? Apsu at her side? A mermaid on the rocks combing her hair? She was none of these, but a slim woman on the wet sand, seeming very young in a man's shirt and calf-length skirt that blew in the wind. What colours they were I don't know, for at night most colours are shades of grey.

Shyly I walked towards her and halted short. I saw her smile, for her teeth caught the moonlight.

"Come." She held out an arm. "Let me see you close."

She stayed still. I was the one who approached.

"Closer," she said and took me by both hands. "So, Duncan McKenzie's other child. We meet again."

I wore my jeans and an anorak. Though my hair is short, she brushed it from my brow and tilted my face to the moonlight.

"Yes. You are very like him. As like as my Apsu."

I don't know what I felt as she touched me: dizzy, privileged, frightened? And though at the back of my mind I remembered all my father had told me – the cruelty, the shipwrecks, the savage white horses – I had no wish to run. All I wanted at that moment was to stay in this woman's company for ever. Thoughts of my mother were wiped away. Neiraa's extraordinary wild beauty, her voice, the touch of her fingers – I, a boy of twelve, was as helpless as my father and the sailors he had spoken about.

"Come, walk with me." She released my hand. "Tell me about – well, your family."

She looked down at me. The breeze blew strands of hair across her face. She drew them back and started along the seashore – in the opposite direction from the beach where I had met Apsu.

The waves tumbled and hissed on the sand.

"Your mother, Jessie, she is at home now?"

I looked up, the top of my head a little above her shoulder. "Yes, with my father."

I heard a soft intake of breath. "I am told she is very beautiful."

"Yes. Or she was until – "

"Until?"

"She had an accident," I said.

"And that spoiled her beauty?"

"It marked her face."

I sensed her smile. "Your mother, then, she is not as beautiful as me?"

"Oh no." Even as I said it I felt a sense of betrayal. "I don't think there's anyone as beautiful as you."

Her hand stroked my hair.

"But then, why does your father stay with her?"

I hesitated. "He – likes her."

"Likes?"

"Well – loves."

"But he loves me!" She halted. "He is my husband!"

"I don't know," I said. "He's my father. He's only just come home."

"Home!" She spat the word. "And instead of me,

Neiraa, he chooses to stay with this – farmwife! This scar-face!"

I hated the way she spoke, the way she had changed. But that did not mean I wanted to be parted from her.

"Please don't," I said.

We walked on.

"And this Jessie," she said, "your mother. She loves him too?"

"Yes," I said. "Very much. She thought he was dead. And he's changed. It's hard for her."

"Which does she love more? You or him?"

"I don't know. I've lived with her all my life, perhaps me. But Dad's just come back. It's different."

"So, you. But how strong is her love? Would she die for you?"

"I don't know," I said again and halted. "Will you stop saying these things. Please!"

She walked on and I had to trot to catch up.

Soon we reached the end of the beach. Before us barnacled rocks rose to the base of a cliff. Above lay the grassy headland.

Abruptly her mood changed and Neiraa smiled. "Never mind." She stepped up and held out a hand. "Let us climb the rocks a little. Look out across the sea."

Feeling very relieved, I followed. Sometimes side by side but more often Neiraa leading the way, we mounted from the beach. Once more the dream was perfect. All the painful questions, all thoughts about my mother and father and home, drifted from my mind. Nothing mattered but now. Continually I lifted my eyes from the rocks to the figure of my companion.

I have said that the moonlight washes out colour, but as we climbed higher and the waves broke below, swilling into the rock pools, I could have sworn that a change came over Neiraa. Her manner was eager. When my foot skidded a little she laughed and grabbed the shoulder of my anorak. For the first time I noticed a dot of ruby light in the depths of each eye.

At length we could go no further, a deep cleft in the rocks barred our progress. I knew it well – indeed, I often went there to fish. Treacherous water lay below us, surging up the walls as the waves rolled in, and falling back in turmoil.

"Look," said Neiraa.

I turned and saw her facing out to sea. Her long loose hair blew in the wind.

"The world of my people. The salt sea, the great oceans – whales, dolphins, islands. Three-quarters of the earth."

She put a hand into her pocket – and suddenly I recognized my mother's skirt, the one that had vanished from the washing line. I didn't mind, it made me smile. Apsu wore my jeans, Neiraa wore Mum's skirt.

As she withdrew her hand I saw that she was holding something.

"What's that?" I said.

She let it unroll, shimmering and sparkling.

"Your silver belt!"

And even then I didn't realize what peril I was in.

"That's right. I believe you saw your brother's." She smiled again, only this time it was different. This time I saw her bottom teeth also. "And when I put it on?"

Her nails were dark against the bright material. "You'll turn back into a sea lady," I said.

She laughed. "So I will, a sea lady. And how would you like to be a sea boy? How would you like to join us in our watery world, our salty hunting-ground?"

"It would be brilliant!" I said. "If you give me one of your belts, will I suddenly grow a tail and be able to swim like Apsu?"

"Of course not!" she said. "You little fool! Did you think I meant as one of the hunters?"

An electric shiver ran through me. I stared at her. Neiraa's face had changed. She was beautiful still, but now it was a savage beauty.

I started back.

She caught me by an arm. Claws dug through my jacket.

"Neiraa!" I shouted. "No!"

"Jessie's brat!" she hissed. "Duncan's earth boy! How I hate you! Did you think you could come down here and make a friend of *me*? Did you imagine in your wildest dreams that I, Neiraa, would feel kindness towards you? You of all people?" She snarled. "No, there's only one end to your visit here tonight."

She dragged me towards the deep cleft in the rocks. Beneath us the black water sucked and surged. I struggled but she was much too strong. It was impossible to break the grip of those claws.

We fought on the brink.

"Now!" cried Neiraa. "Are you ready?"

I clung to her hair, her skirt. She pulled my hands away and flung me forward.

My feet were over the edge.

"No!" I screamed.

Above me Neiraa tugged at the catch of my mother's skirt.

Frantically I scrabbled for a hold but there was nothing. I slipped further. Pebbles pulled out of the earth. The sharp rock cut my hands and face.

Then I was falling – down into the black and foaming gully. With a fountain of spray and a whack that knocked the breath from my lungs, I struck the leaping water. Luckily there was no submerged rock where I landed. The next instant I was sucked out of the gully into the moonlight and flung back in.

High above me, Neiraa still struggled with the catch of her skirt. In her haste the zip had jammed. Furiously she tugged at the waistband. The silver belt fluttered from her hand.

All was water and confusion. The sea sank back and long weed coiled round me. My clothes were heavy. I struggled to stay afloat. Then the waves crashed in and I was thrown against the wall of the gully.

A ledge of rock was before my face. I grabbed it, tearing my fingertips on the barnacles though I didn't feel it until later. This way and that the water buffeted me, then fell back again and I was left hanging.

There was a toe-hold to my right. I managed to swing my leg across.

The next wave crashed in, lifting me with it.

By this time Neiraa had torn open the zip, thrown off her skirt and buckled the shimmering belt around her waist. Like a silver dart she flashed down past me into the tossing water. I felt my foot seized in a grip of steel. But as the sea flooded back out, Neiraa sank with it. My shoe was torn off. With a last slash of her claws my sock too was pulled off and my ankle deeply gashed. Then she was gone.

A succession of small fissures and flakes of rock provided good grips. I scrambled higher. And as the next wave burst into the gully, rebounding from wall to wall, I was beyond Neiraa's reach. She sprang from the water, arms reaching, fingers clawed, but I was half a metre too high and still climbing. My sodden anorak hampered my arms, the jeans twisted round my legs. Despite this, two minutes later I reached the top of the cleft and dragged myself over the brink to safety.

My heart hammered. Somewhere beneath me Neiraa was lost in the shadows and foam. Her voice drifted up:

"You escape this time! Land brat! But I'll be waiting . . . with the black dogs and the white horses . . . for you *and* your ugly mother! You hear? Your father *will* come back with me to the islands!"

She emerged into the moonlight, staring up. Her long hair spread wide. Her shining tail curled in the waves. Even at that moment, shaking with fear, I saw how beautiful she was.

Then I turned and scrambled up the cliff to the headland. It was a track I knew well. And when I looked back, all was at peace: waves murmured on the rocks, the bright beach was deserted, the dappled sea spread round me on three sides.

Neiraa was gone.

# Chapter Eight

# The Rifle and the Pony

Tragedy came to the glen and my family was the cause of it.

Everyone was very kind. Following the loss of our flock we now had no sheep to provide a livelihood. The local crofters held a meeting and it was unanimously agreed – for my mother was well-liked and respected – that each would donate a ewe, with or without a lamb, as the foundation of a new flock. My mother, who took the decisions and acted as head of the family, was reluctant to accept, for our neighbours were not wealthy people. Eventually she was persuaded and now, waiting to be marked, our new flock grazed in a pasture well up the glen, away from the treacherous cliff.

The story of my escape spread rapidly. As it went from house to house, people who had always known freedom became frightened and cautious. Children were kept close to home. Men armed themselves as they went off to work in the fields, though what protection a garden fork or a shotgun would be against Neiraa's enchantment, I do not know. My mother, independent as usual, softened a little candle wax with paraffin and pressed it into cotton-wool. This made very effective earplugs.

"I know it sounds pathetic, earplugs!" she said. "But they worked for your father, and Odysseus's crew in that legend. Anyway, I don't know what else to do."

Magnus, however, had an idea. From some boozing pal at the Clachan Inn he borrowed a .22 rifle and started patrolling the cliffs. In an old rucksack he carried sandwiches and a few cans of beer. He had no job to go to; the weather turned warmer; sometimes he did a bit of fishing. It was a pleasant way to pass the day before the bar opened.

One afternoon he was sitting on the rocks, float bobbing nearby, when he spotted a movement in the water. The sea was calm, he saw it clearly, a hundred metres distant. Wearing his customary overalls, Magnus merged in with the hillside. He froze and quietly set down his can.

The movement came again – a swirl, a small splash, the tip of a big tail. There was no doubt – this was Neiraa, the sea woman, the killer I had told them about. Slowly he picked up the two-two, checked that the magazine was full, the safety-catch off, and set it across his knees. One-handed, he raised his binoculars. Neiraa's head rose above the glassy swell. His intention wavered; like my father and me, like all men who saw her, Magnus was awe-struck by her beauty.

Then just beyond Neiraa he saw another move-ment. The water parted and up came a second head. Even at that distance, with his hair long and sleek, Apsu's resemblance to me was plain to see. Mother and son. My brother! Magnus's resolution almost deserted him. Then he remembered our dead sheep and what had nearly happened to me. His heart hardened. Softly he set down the binoculars and raised the rifle to his shoulder, snuggling his plump cheek against the stock.

Neiraa and Apsu swam closer. Heads above the water, they gazed around like seals.

Suddenly Apsu halted, staring straight at

Magnus. "Myami!" he cried and pointed, then flipped like a dolphin and was gone.

Neiraa was a second behind him. It was too long. As she sprang from the water, Magnus's finger tightened on the trigger.

CRACK – crack!

The sound of the shot whip-cracked across the sea, spat back almost instantaneously from the nearby cliff. In the midst of her dive Neiraa jerked as if she had been kicked and fell back with a cry and a clumsy splash.

But she was not killed, or even seriously hurt. For two heads, at first further away then close at hand among the floating weed and rocks, rose to see who had done this thing. Their eyes were narrow, vengeful. Neiraa's hand covered her shoulder where the bullet had cut a burning gash. Trickles of blood mingled with seawater ran down her white skin. Magnus, standing at the edge of the tide, saw them too late. By the time he had swung his rifle they were gone, sunk into deep water with scarcely a ripple.

By nightfall there was not a family in the glen who did not know Magnus's story. With every dram that slipped down his throat the events grew more dramatic. To some he was a hero. Others said: "Damn

Magnus! Why didn't he leave it to someone who was a better shot."

My father covered his eyes when the news reached him. "Oh, Magnus, you idiot! What have you done! Why didn't you tell me!"

But Magnus was not there to listen. Blear-eyed and happy, slumped on his regular stool in the public bar of the Clachan Inn, he was champion of the hour.

The following morning, predictably, Magnus had a hangover. It did not last beyond lunchtime, however, and in the afternoon he and I walked up the glen to see our new flock and look over the peat banks. Soon it would be time to start cutting.

It was another perfect day. At that time of year there were no flies or maddening midges. Above us the hills were sharp-etched against the sky. The sweet brown river, here and there dammed into pools for trout fishing, ran musically over the rocks.

Beneath my jeans my leg was bandaged halfway to the knee to protect the deep scratches Neiraa had given me. Magnus – fat, lazy, good-natured Magnus – wore a jersey beneath his usual faded overalls, and a thick leather belt on top. The .22 rifle hung comfortably in the crook of his arm.

Our sheep were safe, the peat banks drying out. Far up the glen we sat on the riverbank, enjoying the warmth of the sun after a long winter. High overhead a pair of buzzards wheeled and cried in the blue.

"Look." I pointed down at some minnows, barred and bright at the water's edge.

But Magnus was looking neither up nor down. I followed his gaze. A short distance upstream a pony had emerged from behind a thicket of birch trees. Briefly it stood, looking this way and that, then lowered its muzzle to drink at a grassy pool. It was a pretty animal, light grey, almost white, with a darker mane.

"Have you seen that before?" Magnus said.

I shook my head. But in view of all the strange things that had happened recently, the appearance of the pony gave me a sense of foreboding.

"Let's leave it. Come on." I jumped to my feet and prepared to climb back to the track a hundred metres up the hillside.

"Maybe it's lost." Magnus brushed off some stalks of heather and threw me a square of chocolate.

"You're getting jumpy. I can't blame you, but look at it! What harm can a little pony like that do us?"

I couldn't disagree. It was one of those ponies you can't resist patting. But still – that feeling.

"Anyway." Magnus ran his hand over the two-two. "And you've got your knife, haven't you?"

I tugged the sheath comfortable on my belt. "I suppose you're right."

Nevertheless, I hung behind as Magnus walked up the river.

"Come on, then," he called to the pony. "Tck-tck! Who's a bonny wee fella!"

The pony looked up as he approached. The heavy fringe hung to its eyes.

Again I had that premonition. "Magnus, leave it. There's something wrong. Let's go home."

He ignored me. "Something wrong," he cooed to the pony. "What's he talking about? What could be wrong with a pretty wee fella like you?"

The pony tossed its head then was still as Magnus came up to it and stretched out a hand.

I don't really trust horses. I don't like the way they roll their eyes. I always feel they're planning to bite me with those long yellow teeth.

This pony was different. As Magnus patted its

neck it performed none of the usual threatening gestures, and when it threw up its head, snickering with pleasure, I saw that its teeth were white.

Magnus set his rifle on a tussock of grass a safe distance from the river and caught the pony gently by an ear. It allowed him to do so, mumbling his overall with its soft muzzle. A big granite boulder stood at the pony's side. I had scarcely noticed it previously, but as Magnus released its ear, the pony looked round at this. Had it not been a dumb animal, I would have said it was inviting him to mount.

Magnus followed its gaze. He hesitated, then looked into the pony's face and at its sturdy back.

"No, Magnus!" I stood by a rotting fence post ten metres away. "Don't."

"Why not?" he said. "If it can take my weight. Just a little trot. Shake my dinner down. What harm can I come to up here?"

It made me very uneasy. Biting my lip, I watched him soothe the pony's side and clamber on to the stone. The pony stood still and the next moment he was astride, fingers knotted in the thick grey mane.

"Tck-tck!" He tapped the pony's flanks with his heels.

Obediently it trotted about the grass, turning right and left.

My bandage had come loose and hung in folds about my ankle. I unwound it and pushed it into a pocket. The deep scratches were scabbing over.

The pony walked towards me.

"I haven't been on a horse since I was a boy." Magnus grinned happily. "You'll have to have a shot when I get off." He turned his head. "In fact, why don't you get up behind me, there's plenty of room."

And strange though it seems, there *was* plenty of room, even though the pony was small – maybe not quite as small as I had imagined – and Magnus was a big man.

"No." I retreated behind the lopsided fence post.

"Come on."

I didn't move, even though the pony, as chance would have it, had come to a halt and stood scratching its side on the only short stretch of fence that remained standing, from which I could have mounted very easily.

Its nostrils flared, it looked round at the fence. Then – and had it been human I would have said impatiently – it trotted back to Magnus's mounting-stone and stared directly at me.

"Magnus," I said. "That's enough. Get down now."

"In a minute," he answered. "I'm enjoying this. Tck-tck!" Again he urged the pony forward – but this time it didn't move. "Gee up."

The pony looked back at him with a rolling eye. It gave a little buck.

Magnus clung tight. I was impressed by his horsemanship.

Restless now, the pony pranced sideways. It really was much larger than I had realized. A fore-hoof struck the rifle butt and sent it spinning to the brink of the river.

"Woa! Woa!" Magnus tugged the mane hard. "Hey! Watch the rifle!"

Another hoof struck the barrel. The borrowed two-two rebounded off a stone and splashed into the water.

Things were getting out of hand.

"Ewan!" Magnus's shout was full of alarm. "Get the rifle!"

I ran forward, but the pony's behaviour had become wild. It danced towards me and reared, slashing with sharp hooves. I jumped back.

"Magnus! Let go its mane! Throw yourself on the grass!"

"I can't!"

"What?"

"I can't, Ewan!" I shall never forget his despairing cry. "I can't let go!"

Then I saw – and this time there was no doubt – that no longer was this a small and pretty pony but a full-sized horse, a grey-white stallion. Its mane tossed, its tail flew. Throwing back its head it emitted scream after scream, the terrifying sounds we had heard from the hill on the night our sheep were killed.

"Ewan!" Magnus's shout was almost another scream. "Get the rifle. Shoot it! Shoot it!"

But I could not for the horse, with Magnus clinging to its back, pursued me up and down the riverbank, charging, biting, rearing above my head. Had it not been for rocky outcrops and the thicket of twisted birch trees through which I could dodge, my chance of survival would have been very poor.

Twigs and thorns raked my healing ankle. Blood

ran down into my shoe. I scarcely noticed.

The horse turned its attention from me and trampled the rifle in the river. Time and again it crashed down with its front hooves.

Finally, with poor Magnus shouting for help and being tossed like a sack on its back, the horse galloped off through the heather and dry grass that covered the valley bottom.

I watched it go, leaping a dyke, mane and tail flying, then ran to the stony river and fished out the rifle. The sights were twisted, the trigger jammed. Though I shook out the water and tried my best to fire it, I could not.

Swiftly the horse and its helpless rider drew away down the glen.

I threw off my anorak and scrambled up the slope to the track. As fast as I could with my crippled leg, I ran after them. But by that time Magnus and the horse were far away. A minute later they disappeared behind a fold in the hills.

At the same time one of our neighbours, a sensible man named John Sutherland, was driving his tractor in a high field above the cliffs. He told us what he had seen with his own eyes.

It was the screams, audible even above the

clatter of the engine, which drew his attention. Braking, he looked behind and saw a tremendous white horse, its ears flattened and a rider on its back, racing towards him across the hillside. As it came closer, he was astonished to see that the rider was Magnus. The horse galloped past the field where he was working. Although terrified and shaken half unconscious, Magnus recognized him. "Johnnie!" he shouted. "Johnnie!" And that was all, for the wild neighing of the horse drowned him out and then they were past. They were heading, John saw, straight for the cliff, which at that point was almost at its highest. Quickly he disengaged the machinery he was using and pursued them in the tractor. Though he was still a hundred metres away when the horse reached the crumbling cliff edge, he saw clearly what happened. With a great leap it took off into space and both were falling. Then there was a *crack* like a short peal of thunder – which was heard by several people in the glen. At the same instant the horse was gone, vanished, and Magnus was falling alone. He dropped out of sight and by the time John had stopped his tractor and run to the top of the precipice, Magnus was dead. Below were no rocks, only deep water. It was red,

and in a small tumult he saw an arm, a lashing tail.
Then the water stilled. Slowly the red thinned out
and disappeared.

Magnus was gone.

# Chapter Nine

# Rusty Beacon

No trace of Magnus was found, either that day or in the days and weeks that followed. It was not surprising for the currents are strong and after washing our headlands they run off into the deep waters of the ocean.

Poor Magnus! His death left a gap in my life. For as long as I could remember he had been there like an uncle, an uncle who never quite grew up. I missed him.

I was questioned by the police and the media returned. For three days I knew what it was like to be a hounded celebrity. When we peeped from the window, photographers were there. When my mother bundled me into the car for school, flash

guns went off in our faces. Reporters waited at the
school gates and invaded the playground. It had
been bad enough to see the horse carry Magnus
away; now I became doubly upset and several
times broke down in tears. My mother kept me
from school. Angrily she remonstrated with the
reporters and photographers and in the end they
left me in peace. As it had been after the loss of our
sheep, when there was no fresh news the media
people departed and the glen returned to normal –
or as near normal as was possible in the circum-
stances.

It was decided I should return to school on the
Monday. On the Friday morning prior to this, my
mother drove over to comfort Peter and Johnina
and take them some freshly-baked scones. They
were, though not quite our nearest neighbours, our
best friends, and Magnus – carefree, unemployed,
middle-aged Magnus – had been their only child.

"Take care, Jessie," my father said as she stood
buttoning her coat in the kitchen.

She looked at him in surprise. "I'm only going
over to Johnina's. Surely I'll be safe that far."

"Aye, well." He managed a smile. "Look after
yourself, anyway."

"No fear of that," she said briskly and lifted the white cloth of scones into her basket. "Right, that's me. Back in an hour – or I might nip over to the shop." She picked up the car keys. "And stop brooding. There's plenty needs doing about the place."

"Aye, aye."

"And Ewan," she turned at the door. "I don't want you wandering off. Stay close to the house. Are you listening?"

"I can hear you," I said.

My father followed her outside and stood watching as she turned the car and drove off.

When she had gone I pottered about the out-buildings and did a couple of the odd jobs she had mentioned: tightening some fence wire and removing twigs from the barn roof. I was just coming down the ladder when from the corner of my eye I spotted a movement among the whins above the house. It was just a flash and when I looked directly all was still. It could have been anything, a black lamb or a crow, imagination even, and I thought no more about it.

My father had returned to the kitchen and when I went indoors I found him slumped in a chair at the table, staring into space. Before him a mug of coffee had gone cold, a single bite had been taken from a slice of toast and marmalade.

"Come on, Dad."

I cut a slice of bread for myself and dropped it into the toaster. When I turned round he was regarding me with troubled eyes.

"It's not your fault what happened to Magnus," I said.

He drew a shaky breath. "Aye, Ewan, but it is. Of course it is. Poor Johnina!"

"But Magnus didn't have to – "

"If I hadn't come back none of this would have happened, would it? Your mother's flock, Magnus, nearly you. What if you'd got on that horse's back; hadn't climbed out of that gully?" His eyes fell to my jeans. "Even all those years ago: your injured leg, your mother's face."

I didn't know what to say and was saved by the toaster which at that moment popped up behind me. While I was busy with the butter and black-currant jam, he left the table and went upstairs. I heard him moving about in my room and my mother's. After a few minutes he came back down and wandered aimlessly about the kitchen, straightening little things on the dresser, tipping his coffee down the sink, examining a framed photograph of myself as a little boy. Then, to my surprise, he came behind my chair, pulled my shoulders against him and kissed the top of my head.

"I do love you, Ewan. You'll never know how much."

I looked up. There were tears in his eyes.

"I love you too, Dad."

He nodded, tightening his lips, then squeezed my shoulders and moved away. "A right pair of lassies. Lucky there's no one watching."

Wiping his cheeks with the flat of his hand, he went out into the sunshine.

I sat on at the table wondering what all this meant. Fly wandered in and looked in her bowl for scraps. I gave her a pat, then realized that everything outside was very quiet.

"Dad?"

I ran from the back door. The sheds were deserted. Then I saw him halfway to the shore.

"Dad!"

Fly at my back, I ran down the hillside, climbed a couple of fences and pursued him down the road.

He turned, still a good way off, and shouted. "Away home now, Ewan. You heard your mother, stay near the house. I'll be back in a while."

I stopped. "Where are you going?"

"Never you mind. Just to the shore. Now be a good lad and do as you're told." He walked on.

I watched his back, feeling very uneasy, then trotted after him.

This time he waited and just past the turning place, where the tarmac ends and the track turns left between fields and dunes to the harbour, I came up to him.

"You shouldn't be here," he said. "Didn't you hear me? It's not safe."

"I just want to know where you're going," I said.

"Only to the harbour." He looked away. "Check the mooring. Give the engine a clean up."

I looked at him. "No you're not."

He shrugged guiltily.

"You're going to see *her*, aren't you?"

"Well, somebody has to do something. We can't go on like this."

"But that doesn't mean you have to – "

"I just want to have a word with her. See if I can't persuade her to – "

"But you know you can't. She's not like that. You said: she'll hunt you down and take you back."

"Maybe I was exaggerating a bit."

"After what she did to Magnus? No you weren't. All she has to do is start that singing and there's nothing you can do about it."

He looked at me sideways. "Isn't there? What about those things your mother gave us for putting in our ears?"

"The earplugs?" My heart gave a little jump. "Are you telling the truth? Are you really just going to *talk* to her? And if she starts the singing you'll – " I gestured – "so she won't be able to take you away?"

"Of course." He patted his pocket. "I'm not daft. Do you think I'd just go off again? Leave you and your mother?"

"Oh, Dad!" I took his arm. "But you'll have to be quick."

"Like lightning." He smiled. "Now go on back to the house. I'll see you in a while."

"Can I not come with you? Apsu might be there." I felt in my jeans pocket and showed him my own earplugs; Mum made me carry them. "She won't hurt me while you're around."

"No." He shook his head. "Absolutely not."

"Why?"

"Just not, that's all. I don't want you there. Now go on up to the house like you're told. Your mother will be back soon."

I began to feel suspicious again. "No, I'm coming."

"Ewan! Do you want me to get cross?"

"I don't care," I said. "You can get as cross as you want. I'm coming anyway. I'll follow you. You can't stop me."

My father seized me by the jersey and raised his hand. We were both startled and a moment later he let go again.

"Now away home!"

"No."

He sighed. "Your mother said you were thrawn. All right, if you're coming, you're coming. There's no point fighting about it." He looked towards the harbour. "But when we get there you do exactly as I say – and I mean it. All right?"

"Yes, Dad."

The track was stony with a strip of car-beaten grass in the middle. Side by side we walked on.

Roughly midway between the tarmacked road

and the harbour, rooks and gulls were mobbing something in the field. The air was loud with their clamour. As we came closer Fly, who had been trotting around us, suddenly growled and drew back, staring towards the birds.

"What is it, girl?" I followed her gaze.

She growled again, showing her teeth. Then she turned and silently, in that low-belly collie run she used on the hill, fled back the way we had come. In seconds she was gone.

Normally I would have laughed and said that Fly had the spooks again. Now I gave a shiver.

The drystone dyke prevented us from seeing what it was in the field that had frightened her and so excited the birds. Whatever it was, it was very tempting, for Dad and I were almost upon them before the birds ceased their squabbling and retreated a few metres until we had passed. A last gull flew up, something pink and shining in its beak, and was pursued by others. With loud cries, diving and dodging, they flew off.

Apprehensively I jumped the ditch and looked over the wall. A pretty brown and white calf lay beyond. It was not a day dead, maybe much less, for its coat was clean and, though it may have been imagination, I thought I could smell warm flesh. Its eyes were gone and there was a hole in its belly, but these I had seen often enough. What I had not seen, however, and drew my alarmed gaze, were the terrible wounds in its neck. This calf had not died a natural death, it had been killed and my thoughts leaped to memories of our sheep, and the white horse with Magnus on its back, and the dog which had attacked me seven years earlier.

My father joined me. Together we looked all round, from the grassy dunes to rocks and other drystone dykes and thorny thickets on the hillside. I drew my sheath knife and my father twisted a sharp baton of wood from a tangle of rusty wire. Thus armed, we stood on the track. The harbour, with a little stone shed for storing gear – oars and nets, outboards and oilskins – was two minutes away; the house was six or eight. We ran to the harbour.

But no carnivorous horse or savage black dog appeared to confront us. Side by side we stood on the L-shaped jetty. Out on the water the *Kittiwake* and three more open boats rocked at their moorings. Long lines, their colours faded, led to ringbolts at our feet. Stacks of creels and fish boxes lay in the shelter of the sea wall, which ran the full length of the jetty.

"Well, it seems safe enough." My father threw aside his weapon. "At least nothing can surprise us here."

He looked inland, and having satisfied himself that the hillside was clear, shaded his eyes to stare along the coast. I followed his gaze. My eyes are keen. Nothing unfamiliar disturbed the scene: no splash of a big fish tail, no head bobbing in the waves. Only a seal rose to gaze around, gulls cried, cormorants dived from the nearby rocks.

Between the shed and the outer end of the jetty a flight of stone steps led to the top of the sea wall. We climbed them. The view from that point was tremendous, three hundred and sixty degrees: each way along the coast, inland to the mountains, and seaward to Roan Island, three miles offshore, and the horizon beyond.

"You stay here." My father indicated the top of the steps. "It's safer. Keep your eyes skinned. If you see anything, give me a shout and run like hell to the shed."

He turned from me and walked to the end of the sea wall where a broken beacon, two metres high and ringed by an iron rail, stood rusting above the entrance to the harbour. Standing in that exposed spot, he scanned the water, then put fingers to his mouth and blew a long strange whistle.

He waited. And I waited. The breeze blew my hair. The waves rolled in as before.

He repeated the whistle. And gave it again.

I searched the hillside, and standing back from the edge, for there was no safety rail, looked down at the water. Though I loved the harbour, this was a spot that had always frightened me. When the tide is out, bare rocks lie to the seaward side of the wall; but at other times, even on calm days, the waves splash up and the current flows faster than a man can swim. Now, five or six metres beneath me, the tide was rising. The water looked cold. Bubbles and foam drifted past and were carried out to sea in a winding ribbon.

Fifteen minutes passed. Half an hour. My father returned and we descended the steps to the jetty.

"They must be away hunting," he said. "Otherwise she would have come. Unless – " His face had taken on the wild, frightened look it had when he first returned. "I wish you hadn't come, Ewan. I wish you'd stayed at home or gone back like I told you."

"What do you mean?" I said. "Unless what?"

"Unless – well, perhaps she's seen me and thinks it looks like a trap. Perhaps she thinks I might go out to her in the boat. She could be waiting for me out on the island right now, with Apsu. No people, no guns, a place to talk."

I looked across the water. "You won't go?"

After a moment he said, "What if I did, Ewan?"

"You can't! You know what'll happen. Remember what you were like when you came back. And we'd never see you again. You *said*, there'll not be another ship."

"You don't have to remind me. But what kind of man risks the life of his wife and son? Twice you've had a narrow escape – three times if you count that evening you met Apsu. What about the next time – and the next? How long do you expect your luck to hold out?"

"But if you go – what about Mum and me?"

"What about you if I don't go?"

My chest was tight. Angrily I felt tears spring to my eyes and kicked a ringbolt hard.

"I've got to talk to her, you must see that. She won't hurt me. And like I said," he tried to smile, "there's always your mum's earplugs."

He walked a few paces and bent to the slack orange mooring line that ran from the *Kittiwake* to the jetty.

"No, Dad, don't!" I ran across and pulled at his arm. "You can borrow a rifle, like Magnus, and shoot her."

He straightened. "Shoot her, so easy. And what about Apsu, your brother? He's my son too, you know. How would you feel if I shot *your* mother?"

I was silenced and stood watching as he loosened the rope and pulled the *Kittiwake* from her mooring to the foot of a rusty metal ladder set into the jetty.

" 'Bye then, Ewan. Wish me luck. I'll try not to be too long." He gave me a rough hug, pressing my head to his shoulder. "Stay at the harbour here, don't risk walking home. Somebody will be along in a while." He let go of me and abruptly turned away.

I wanted to rush at him, drag him back, smash boulders into the *Kittiwake* until she sank. Instead, I watched numbly as my father descended the iron ladder, and for the first time noticed that his hair was thinning slightly on the crown. The boat rocked as he stepped aboard and pulled the cover from the outboard. Details have stuck in my mind: the way he pushed off with an oar against the jetty wall; the boat drifting out stern-first into the harbour; his hands lean and brown as he adjusted the choke; the *whirr, whirr, whirr* as the temperamental engine failed to fire, then roar and cloud of blue smoke as it burst into life.

He settled himself at the stern, opened the throttle, and pushed the tiller across. The engine note picked up. The boat swung. Slowly gathering speed, it headed across the harbour. The rippled wake fanned out and lapped the stones below me.

I thought he was not going to look back, then he did, his face pale against the water. But he didn't raise a hand or wave, and a moment later the boat rounded the jetty into the deep water of the channel and he was gone.

I raced up the steps to the top of the sea wall and ran to the rusting beacon at the end. The *Kittiwake* passed beneath me, a dozen metres distant.

"All right, then!" I shouted. "Go on! Go back to her! See if Mum and I care. We managed fine without you before. I wish you'd never come back!"

He heard me but he didn't look up. And it wasn't true at all. Even as I called out, I felt sick at myself and knew I would miss him terribly.

At each side of the channel, long dark weed like tresses of hair curled and coiled and straightened as the waves rose and fell. The boat drew away, gently pitching and rolling as it met the first waves of the open sea.

Briefly I thought of yelling to attract my father's attention, then jumping, forcing him to come back and rescue me. But in an instant all such thoughts were driven from my mind. From the corner of my eye I glimpsed something moving and turned to see.

A huge black dog, big as a six-week-old calf, walked slowly on to the jetty. Which way it had approached, I have no idea. Its coat was ragged. A red tongue lolled from powerful jaws. The dog halted, staring towards me at the end of the sea wall.

Instantly, after seven years, I recognized it. Fear made me tingle from my legs to the crown of my head.

The dog sensed it and wrinkled its lips in a silent snarl. I saw the savage teeth.

"Dad!" I shouted. "Dad!" But still he did not turn. Perhaps my voice no longer reached him above the roar of the engine.

I looked all round. There was no retreat. The

stone shed, my only refuge, stood below me on the jetty, midway between the dog and myself. To reach it I had to run along the sea wall, descend twelve steps, and dash to the entrance. The door was open, I could wedge it shut from inside. But unless I got a long start, halfway at least, the dog would easily reach the shed before me, and then –!

For the second time that morning I pulled my knife from its sheath. Moving slowly, I advanced along the sea wall.

To begin with all went well. The dog stood watching. But as I reached the top of the steps, almost as if it sensed my intention, it started forward. I halted but the dog did not. A stiff-legged walk became a trot and then a bounding run. I fled back along the wall. In two or three leaps the dog was up the stone steps and on the sea wall behind me.

I ran to the far side of the beacon and grasped the rusty rail. Now it had me cornered, and perhaps seeing the bright blade in my hand, the dog halted. Again it snarled, this time deep in its throat. With narrowed yellow eyes it watched me, then resumed that slow, stiff-legged walk of a dog which is ready to attack.

Three metres apart, the dog and I stared at each

other. Its back was as high as my waist. Even in that exposed location I smelled the animal stink from its black coat.

With no warning it sprang at me round the beacon. In the same split second I struck out with the knife and dodged to the far side. The blade went home for I felt it jar and with a yowl the dog drew back. Blood ran from a wound in its shoulder.

This did not stop it. Slowly again it closed in and began to track me round the beacon. We had gone only a few paces when abruptly it bounded forward and almost in the same movement doubled back to meet me face to face. A second time I struck out but in the panic of the moment I lost balance and my wrist struck the beacon rail full force. Instantly my hand was numbed. The knife fell from my grasp, bounced once and rattled to the jetty below. And I was driven out from the shelter of the beacon on to the open sea wall.

I had, somehow, wounded the dog again and it paused, rubbing a torn ear with its forepaw. But only for a moment. And now I was helpless. There was no way, even if I sprinted, I could reach the safety of the shed before being pulled to the ground. Head outstretched, dripping blood and showing those terrible teeth, the black dog came towards me. I backed. It gave a spring.

With a despairing cry I threw myself from the sea wall. The waves leaped up. With a smash I struck the water. Icy cold, it closed over my head. In a froth of bubbles I kicked out and bobbed to the surface. High above me, feet planted at the edge, the black dog stared down. It did not follow. Then I felt myself gripped by the current. Waves surged up the wall and fell back. The barnacled stones slipped past. I struggled to hold on but my right hand was dead and there was nothing to grip. Then the beacon was above me. The sea wall was gone. With a swirl and a rush I was carried out into the channel and the deep water beyond.

## Chapter Ten

# The Fight
# For My Father

In a loch or a sheltered bay of the sea I am a good swimmer, but as the current bore me away I thought I would be drowned. My feet were dragged down by shoes, my jeans clung tight, my jersey washed up around my ears. "Help!" Briefly I panicked. "Dad!" Waves swilled over my head and I swallowed mouthfuls of seawater.

Somehow I forced the panic down. Taking a shaky breath, I doubled in the water and managed to wrench off my shoes. They sank into the darkness beneath me. After a second struggle, my jersey too was consigned to the sea.

Now, instead of wallowing, my body rose and fell with the waves. But it was mid-tide and the current was flowing strongly. By the time I was ready to start swimming, I had been carried a hundred metres from shore and nearly as far down-current from the harbour mouth. Beneath me the water was deep, then shallow and broken as I was swept across a rocky outcrop. I reached down with my foot and touched bottom, then a wave lifted me and I was carried on.

A short distance ahead two barnacle-covered peaks of rock still rose above the surface. In the strongest crawl I could manage, I struck out for the nearer. And I almost reached it, but a twist of the current caught me at the last moment and swept me past. All about the outcrop strands of weed like leather straps coiled and shone. I clutched with my left hand but they slipped through my fingers. Then the last tip was gone, the rocks were behind me. Ahead lay open water. Desperately I tried to swim back but it was hopeless. Five metres, ten metres, the water opened between us. "No!" I shouted. "No!" Then a wave washed over my head and I inhaled salt water. Coughing and gasping, I struggled to stay afloat. The current carried me on.

At what moment my father spotted my plight I'm not sure, but I shall never forget the overwhelming relief I felt when, from the rising crest of a wave, I saw the *Kittiwake* heading towards me. In two or three minutes – endless minutes, they seemed – it was at my side. He cut the engine. In the sudden silence I heard the waves slap the planking. Then my father was reaching towards me. "Come on, let's have you." With a strong grip he caught my outstretched hand, my arm, the back of my jeans. Like an ungainly fish, I slithered over the side and landed face-down in the bottom of the boat. Never was the stink of petrol and stale fish so welcome.

Shivering with fright and regaining my breath, I lay where I was, then pulled myself to a seat. My father sat facing me. His face was taut and anxious.

"Lucky you saw me," I said at length. "I'd never have got ashore. The tide was too strong."

"No," he agreed. "What the hell happened?"

"It was the black dog." I looked back at the harbour but the sea wall was empty. The beast that a second time had almost cost me my life was gone.

"The black dog!" He followed my gaze.

I told him my near escape.

"And you could easily have drowned. Oh, Ewan! But you're all right? Your hand?"

The feeling was coming back. I moved my fingers and a fiery pain shot up my wrist. Cautiously I bent it and probed with my other hand. "Nothing broken. A bit sore. No, I'm OK."

My father was troubled. "Do you understand now why I've got to see her. What if I hadn't spotted you? What'll it be the next time?"

"I kept expecting her to come up beside me in the water," I said. "Feel her claws catch my leg and drag me under."

"Don't!" he said, and reached to his feet for the starting cord. "We've got to get you back to the harbour – fast. If she's in the water she'll have heard the engine, even if she's five miles away."

He hooked the toggle of the cord into the slot on the flywheel and wrapped it round three times. Then bracing his hand on the stern, he heaved with all his strength.

WHIR-R-R!

"Damned thing! It's even worse when it's hot. If only I'd come down yesterday and –"

He wrapped it again, braced his legs and *tugged*.

WHIR-R-R, POP!

A third time he wound the cord – then suddenly froze.

At the same instant I heard it myself, Neiraa's voice. Crystal notes, haunting, beautiful, filled the air about us and drifted across the water. I could not tell from what direction they came. Quickly I looked right and left along the coast and out to sea, but saw no sign of Neiraa. Already my hand was deep in my wet pocket and I pulled out Mum's earplugs.

My father, meanwhile, had started singing at the top of his voice.

"La – la – la-la – la!"

He finished winding the starting cord and gave it a wild pull.

WHIR-R-R, POP-POP!

"Ewan, I can't!" he cried. "I can't start it! La – la-la – la-la – la – "

Then the world went dead and muffled as I shook off the seawater and squashed the wax into my ears.

My father stared around and he was shouting but I couldn't make out the words. Then he clapped both hands over his ears and I saw his tongue and the morning stubble dark on his cheeks as he sang on, harsh and deep and tuneless.

"Your earplugs!" My voice came from far away as I pointed to my pocket and mimed pressing them into my ears. "Put them in!"

He can't have heard the words, though I shouted, but he understood me perfectly. Yet he took no action, his hands remained clamped to his ears. Wide-eyed, he gazed at me.

His expression revealed the truth. He had *not* brought the earplugs with him. He had lied to me. From the very start that morning, as he said good-bye to my mother, and hugged me, and wandered through the house, he had intended to go back to his sea wife and their son. He had decided already to sacrifice his freedom for our safety.

I was stunned. I did not want my father to go. I could not bear the thought of Neiraa taking him away a second time, and for ever, just when I was getting to know him.

I tried to pull myself together. It was no good just waiting for it to happen. Was there anything *I* could do to prevent it?

One thing was obvious. He might not be able to use his hands to restart the engine, but I could. Kneeling on the bottom boards, I reached past him and rewound the starting cord. With my left hand I heaved.

The boat heeled. Sluggishly the engine turned over.

I wound it again.

Whirr.

I would never start it, my left arm was not strong enough. But I could row, even with my sore right hand. Quickly I clambered to the centre thwart, dropped the rowlocks into their holes, and took up the oars.

I have been in boats all my life and row well. Trying not to feel the hurt, I turned the *Kittiwake* towards the harbour and pulled with all my strength.

By this time we were six or eight hundred metres down-current, though less than that from shore. Slowly the rocks slid past. My father tipped the engine to lift the propellor from the water and lessen the drag. For a second he stopped singing to listen, then clasped his hands back over his ears.

But though her song filled the air, there was still no sign of Neiraa. As I heaved on the oars, I looked to right and left. The waves were unbroken.

Two hundred metres passed. Suddenly, with no warning, the boat dipped violently and I gave a cry. A strong hand, tipped with claws, appeared on the gunnel and my brother Apsu emerged from the sea. His long black hair was sleek as a seal. As he saw his father – my father – his face lit up. His lips moved, though I couldn't make out the words, and he reached across to take my father's arm. Half a metre of silver tail slid from the water. My father smiled, his eyes full of affection. Briefly he took a hand from his ear to squeeze Apsu's shoulder, and he kissed him on his wet head.

A lump rose in my throat and I felt my eyes pricking again. Not knowing what else to do, I pulled on the oars.

My father looked from Apsu to me, then sharpened his gaze on something ahead of the boat. I turned to see.

Close to a pale outcrop of rocks, Neiraa had broken the surface. Slim arm outstretched, she balanced among the swishing weed and watched as I rowed past. Despite all that I had heard, she was as lovely, as fascinating as ever. The cut of Magnus's bullet was dark on her shoulder, but already it was healing. Her lips curved in a perfect smile, her eyes sparkled. Rising and sinking as the waves rolled in, she opened her mouth in song.

At the same time, Apsu leaned close to speak to my father, but my father would not listen and kept both hands pressed to his ears. Apsu pleaded, his face intense. He gripped my father's wrist and attempted to drag his hand away.

At this, *I* began to sing, my voice like a corncrake: loudly, anything, nonsense words to drown out the song of Neiraa. Lifting an oar in both hands, I slashed it down at my brother's back.

From the corner of his eye Apsu saw me and flung himself backwards into the water. The oar missed him and struck the stern with a splintering thud.

I looked towards the rocks. Neiraa was gone. My father stared at me. He was speaking. I couldn't hear but I knew what he was saying: I shouldn't have done it; Apsu was my brother; I had made Neiraa angry.

I resumed rowing, but the boat was barely moving again when one of my oars was seized from the water. I could not move it. Neiraa clung to the blade. I tugged but it was torn from my hand and flung aside with a splash.

The *Kittiwake* drifted to a halt, rocking in the waves. Furiously Neiraa gazed up at me. I struck at her with the second oar. She dodged quickly and stayed just out of reach, her elegant tail curling in the water. I lashed out at Apsu. He was much too fast. Weapon raised, I waited for a second chance.

But my father was shouting. I looked at him. He had taken his hands from his ears and was telling me to stop. Neiraa and Apsu rocked in the waves. I struck a warning blow at the water. The boat dipped as my father rose. Gently but firmly he took the oar from me and laid it along the side.

As he regained his seat, Apsu swam close to speak to him. Neiraa followed. I reached up to remove one of my earplugs but my father shook his head. Resting a hand on Neiraa's slim arm, he pointed earnestly from me to the harbour. Apsu glanced up with a smile and nodded, but when Neiraa looked towards me her eyes were full of hatred.

It was not difficult to interpret what they were saying. If Neiraa and Apsu would allow me to be set ashore, my father would go with them. It was almost what he had planned from the start, his departure in exchange for my safety. Apsu agreed, Neiraa did not.

Briefly they argued. Neiraa grew angry and raked her nails down the side of the boat, tugging up flakes of paint and splinters of wood. But Apsu refused to yield. Grasping his mother by the shoulders, he shook her. And at length, with bad grace and a scowl, she agreed.

"No!" I shouted. "Dad, no!"

But there was nothing I could do. He said something, I think about keeping the bargain, and was reassured.

For a long time, anxiously, he looked at me and tried to smile, then lowered his eyes to his sea wife and their son.

His hand rested on Apsu's neck. Neiraa took his arm. Smiling again and lovely, she murmured to him and sang softly, as if it were a lullaby.

I watched my father slip away. Little by little the tension and distress drained from his face and was replaced by an expression of such joy and peace that he was transfigured.

Though I could have reached out and touched him, my father was gone, gone from my mother and me and the glen, as surely as if he were already landing on a golden shore of the islands that are not on any map.

# Chapter Eleven

# Walls of Water

Apsu reached over the side of the *Kittiwake* and handed me the missing oar. With a heavy heart I took it. I could not row, however, for in the struggle a rowlock had been knocked into the water. When Apsu realized this, he flipped in a dive to search for it on the sea bed.

My father gestured for me to take out the earplugs. "It's all right," he said as I did so and the sudden noises of the sea and breeze and gulls beat against my eardrums. "She won't sing you away. But why don't you come with us, Ewan?" He leaned closer. "I don't know why I told you all those things before, they were a lot of nonsense. Come with us to the islands. You'll have a wonderful time: sunshine, sea, endless freedom." He smiled. "No school, no homework. It's so beautiful: swimming in the lagoon, fires on the beach at night, all those stars. And fruit – you've never imagined such fruit!" He took my hand. "Come with us. You and Apsu. Everything will be just perfect."

Perfect? I thought about his madness, and games with white skulls; Neiraa striking me into the gully; the lashing tail and red water when Magnus went over the cliff.

"What about Mum?" I said coldly. "What about her?"

"She'll be all right. She's got lots of friends. Probably she'll marry again. Don't worry about your mother, think about yourself."

This was not my father, not Duncan McKenzie speaking, I realized that. Under Neiraa's spell he was helpless. I could not blame him, yet it seemed like treachery. I was sickened.

Just then Apsu rose from the sea. The rowlock was lost. I was not surprised in view of all the rocks and weed beneath us. Also the current had swept us on and we were quite a long way from shore.

"I'll try to start the engine then," my father said, and added hopefully, "if you're absolutely *sure* you don't want to come with us. You're making a big mistake. It would be an adventure!"

"No," I said. "I don't want to go with you. Start the engine."

The sparking plug was soaking. He dried it with a cloth and turned the engine a few times to drive out any petrol that had gathered in the cylinder. Then he dropped the propeller into the water and tinkered with the carburettor. For two or three minutes his back was towards me. This gave me an idea. Once the engine was going, perhaps I could take my father ashore myself. He would soon come to his senses. We could move away from the glen, start life afresh in some place far from the sea, where Neiraa would never find us.

Setting his feet, my father gave the starting cord a hard pull. At once, shockingly loud, the engine burst into life. Carefully he adjusted the choke, settled himself at the stern and opened the throttle. The engine note picked up. Beneath us the propeller churned.

As we returned along the shore, gathering speed and bouncing on the waves, the breeze flowed past. In my wet shirt and jeans I was frozen and clasped arms across my stomach. My father handed me his jersey and opened his own shirt to the waist. I was reminded of the time I had watched him swimming and for a moment thought he was going to take off all his clothes and dive over the side. But he didn't. "Aahhhh!" With a deep sigh of contentment he made himself comfortable and trailed a hand in the water. Then smiling, he threw back his head and closed his eyes as if he was flying.

The sea wall came closer. Soon they would set me ashore. Though it seemed we were going quite fast, Apsu and Neiraa kept pace alongside with lazy sweeps of their tails.

My father glanced sideways and exchanged smiles with his sea wife, adjusted our course a fraction and closed his eyes again.

I sat up and softly took a grip on one of the oars. What I was going to do I scarcely dared think about. But it was now or never. Soon we would be turning into the harbour channel; then my father would be alert. Acting before Neiraa or Apsu had time to shout a warning, I raised the oar and struck my father across the side of the head.

He jerked, his limbs sprawled and he fell limp across the outboard. What I had done horrified me. But there was no time to think for his weight pushed the tiller hard across and the boat heeled out of control. Exerting all my strength, I heaved him to the bottom boards and bound his wrists hastily with an end of rope.

Neiraa and Apsu darted forward. If the boat had kept a steady course, they might have jumped aboard and overpowered me with their strength and long nails. But the *Kittiwake* spun dizzily in circles, bouncing on the waves, and the racing propellor could have cut them badly. Quickly I clambered past my father's limp body and took his place in the stern. Thrusting the throttle full open, I pulled the *Kittiwake* out of her spin and raced for the harbour.

I was not to escape so easily. Neiraa and Apsu, swimming so fast they could have leaped clear across the boat, seized the bow and turned the *Kittiwake* out to sea. One after another they appeared at the sides – now port, now starboard – and snatched for an oar. Their intention, I think, was to thrust it into the propellor and snap off the blades, which would have left me completely at their mercy. My right hand was on the tiller; in my left was the long boathook, sharpened to double as a gaff to heave big fish aboard. Each time they appeared I lashed out clumsily. Thud! Rattle! My weapon hit the side of the boat. Had it hooked either of them in an arm or the back, it could have caused a serious wound.

But from my seat at the engine I could not reach the bow, and however hard I strove to turn the *Kittiwake* back to shore, they kept her heading for the open sea. The rocks and beaches sank behind. Half a mile, a mile of tossing water separated me from the safety of the harbour.

Then I saw that Neiraa had swum aside. White shoulders clear of the waves, she stared up at the sky and lifted her arms. Right and left she turned and threw back her head. I saw her lips moving, but above the roar of the engine and slap of the sea I could hear nothing. What was she doing? Then even as I watched, I felt the breeze freshen and was surprised to see a bank of dark cloud rolling up from the north-west.

Apsu appeared at my side. I struck at him – once, twice. He sank into the water. I threw the tiller across. The boat swung. Apsu's hand caught the bow and turned the *Kittiwake* back out to sea.

I looked astern at his mother. She was still invoking the storm – how wild I could not guess. It rose quickly. Already the breeze had become a stiff wind and the waves were mounting. Half the sky was eaten up by ominous cloud.

My father stirred. His eyes opened. Dazed and confused, he stared at the struts of the pitching boat then up at me. He tugged at his wrists. "What – what's happening?" He struggled to a sitting position.

Neiraa had returned. Like a dolphin she sprang into the air to look down into the boat.

The throttle was pushed wide. The water at the stern boiled in the thrust of the propeller. A ragged wake spread behind us in the tumbling waves. I pushed the tiller hard to starboard, then to port, to make Apsu's job more difficult.

"Ewan! What have you done!" My father stared at me.

"You're not going!" I shouted above the roar of the engine. "I don't care what they do! You're staying here with Mum and me!"

"But I want to go, you little fool! Don't you understand that!" He struggled against the rope. "Let me go!"

Then I saw that his eyes had slipped sideways, looking beyond me. I turned. Neiraa had risen at my shoulder and was listening. Her hand grasped the boat's side and she was being towed in the froth of the propeller. Why she had not attacked me I don't know. For the sake of my father who was watching at that time? To let the storm overwhelm us? She smiled at his words. I raised the boathook. In an instant she was gone.

A white-crested wave gave the *Kittiwake* a buffet. The wind whipped spray across my face.

"Ewan, I'm so sorry!" My father's expression had changed. "I did try to stop you coming. There's nothing we can do now. Whatever happens, it's up to them."

I stared at him. Five minutes earlier he had been trying to persuade me to leave the glen, desert my mother and go away with him. Had the bang on his head released him from Neiraa's spell?

"Apsu made her promise we'd take you back to the harbour," he said. "But now – anything might happen."

He held out his wrists and fell as another wave knocked the boat sideways. I untied the rope. Clinging to a seat, he looked all round. The leaping water rose above us. Far astern, the harbour was hidden in spray. "Try to get you ashore," he said. "Your safety, that's the first thing." Awkwardly we changed places and he took the tiller. "Not a hope of getting back. See if we can make it out to Roan Island."

I looked where he nodded. A mile ahead the rocky island with its sheltered white beach rose above a foaming wave and vanished as we sank into the trough behind. No one lived there but I had known it all my life. This was where my father had met Neiraa and fallen in love all those years ago.

The wind blew harder still. The waves grew rougher. In minutes the gentle sea had been transformed into a tumult. Laughing with excitement, Apsu balanced as the waves rolled by, spray whirling from their crests. From horizon to horizon the sky was inky black. Lightning fizzed from the base of thunder clouds. Rain drove horizontally into our faces. Now there was no need for Apsu to guide the boat's head; if we were not to be swamped there was only one direction to go, bow-first into the waves, further and further out to sea.

My father, who had worked all his life in boats until Neiraa took him away, handled the engine perfectly, nursing us up the long, foam-streaked slopes of the waves and down into the troughs beyond. Yet despite his expert seamanship, we began to take on water. Spray cascaded on our heads; waves splashed over the gunnel. I reached into a locker and pulled out the old five-litre jam tin we used as a baler. The water sloshed about my shins. Working to a rhythm, I flung scoop after scoop over the side: twenty – fifty – a hundred. The water in the boat grew deeper. The little *Kittiwake* was not designed for conditions like this. Steadily, as the storm grew wilder, she was filling up. Her movements grew sluggish.

Neiraa looked down on us from the high crest of a wave. She saw that my father was no longer under her spell. It did not matter, we were still in her power; we were being overwhelmed by the storm.

Beside her in the foam I imagined I saw a shape, leaping and alive. I shifted the focus of my eyes and realized that all about us were white horses – not the mere sea spray that people *call* white horses, but real animals with tossing manes, like the horses that had driven our sheep over the cliff and carried poor Magnus to his death. Their wild eyes looked from the waves, powerful legs plunged and swam beneath them. Neiraa, wilder than any, hung an arm about their necks and waited for the *Kittiwake* to capsize and cast my father and me into the roaring sea.

I baled on, my arms aching. Skilfully my father guided the boat through the waves, drawing ever closer to the safety of Roan Island.

Neiraa realized his intention, that his single wish now was to save me, and minute by minute he came closer to achieving it; that he no longer wished to return to her islands; that all at once she was nothing to him but an enemy who threatened his family. Her laughter faded. Leaving the white horses, she plunged headlong down the side of a wave and struck at me over the side of the boat. Her nails flashed past my face. I sprang back and hit out with the tin. She fell with a splash then leaped from the sea again. The baler was knocked from my grasp, her long nails fastened in my shirt. I tried to tug it away and it tore, but she was strong. My head and shoulders were dragged over the side. I cried aloud. The *Kittiwake*, tossed by the storm, rocked dangerously.

My father left the engine and came to my aid. Drawing back his arm, he struck Neiraa a tremendous blow across the side of the face. She screamed and let go. I felt his hand grab my belt and heave me back into the boat.

I slithered to the deck. The seawater surged

round me, mixed with bottom boards, tangled lines and other debris. Struggling to regain my balance, I looked up. My father's head was raised, a look of horror on his face. I followed his gaze. A wall of white water and galloping horses was descending upon us. In saving me from Neiraa, he had lost control of the boat. I just had time to wrap my arms round a seat, then it struck. Instantly my world was reduced to crashing water and confusion. We were sinking, I was sure of it.

Miraculously we did not. The towering wave passed and the brave little *Kittiwake* was still afloat – just. The engine had been swamped. Nine-tenths full, the boat wallowed heavily in a trough of the waves. High above us, balancing in the watery hillsides, I saw Neiraa and Apsu. Beyond them were the leaping wave crests, the shrieking wind, and black clouds that turned the midday dim.

My father joined me in the bottom of the boat. "Sorry, Ewan." He put an arm about me and I felt his rough whiskers against my face. "I did try."

Then another wave descended upon us, the boat was gone and we were torn apart.

It did not last long, the sense of drowning: water

and panic and pressure; a burning in my chest; pain; then my senses drifting and my limbs falling slack as the sea invaded my throat.

When I opened my eyes again I did not, for quite a time, know where I was.

I lay on sand, the sky was blue, a sweet wind blew from the rippled sea.

My chest was bare; indeed, I wore only my underpants. On a rock nearby my shirt and jeans lay spread to dry.

Coughing, I sat up and looked about me. It was a pretty bay. Apsu, a boy like myself with sturdy legs and no fish's tail, clambered on the nearby rocks. My father, his clothes shared with Neiraa, lay with his head in her lap. She smoothed his wet hair and he smiled up at her.

Somehow, it seemed, I had been transported to the islands of the sea people. Then standing, I saw the *Kittiwake*, her engine gone, rocking at the end of a rope a dozen metres offshore. And three miles across the water I recognized the silhouette of a mountain above our glen, and the beacon on the sea wall of the harbour. This was not the enchanted islands of coconut palms, trade winds and shipwreck, it was Roan Island. And the storm had passed.

I won't linger on the details of my father's departure.

It was my brother Apsu, who came and sat with me, who had saved me from drowning and brought me ashore. Indeed, it was he and not my father, at this time, who showed me care and affection.

My father did love me, I know that, and he loved my mother too. But again he was helpless under Neiraa's spell.

Once I had recovered they did not stay long. My father kissed me and sent a message home but his thoughts ran on ahead. Eagerly he splashed out to the *Kittiwake* and threw the mooring rope to his sea son. Expertly Apsu tied two loops then raised his hands to his mouth and blew a long note. A moment later there was a plunging out at sea and a small herd of white horses came swimming and galloping to shore. He threw the rope over the heads of two and fastened the silver belt about his waist.

Then the whole procession, with scarcely a backward glance, pulled out from the beach. The horses towed, while others leaped alongside and white birds swooped overhead.

I watched them go. What, I thought, of Magnus, and poor lost sailors, and mobiles of skeletons clicking in the wind? The irresistible Neiraa and Apsu criss-crossed beneath the boat and clung to the sides. While in the midst my father, standing like a charioteer with his shirt billowing behind, called encouragement to the horses and fixed his eyes on the horizon as if he followed a vision.

There was great alarm in the glen at my disappearance, particularly in the wake of such a sudden and devastating storm, which blew in windows and ripped the roofs off barns. The *Kittiwake* was missed from her mooring. Searchers combed the shore for a night and a day. But it was my mother, with binoculars, who spotted me on the far white beach of Roan Island. And my mother, in a borrowed boat with Fly standing in the bow, who rowed three miles through the treacherous currents to bring me home.